MODEL BEHAVIOR

An Instalove Age-Gap Romance

Nichole Rose

CONTENTS

Dedication — V

About the Book — 1

Chapter One — 3

Chapter Two — 15

Chapter Three — 25

Chapter Four — 39

Chapter Five — 50

Chapter Six — 67

Chapter Seven — 80

Chapter Eight — 92

Epilogue — 99

Author's Note — 107

Ice Breaker — 108

Instalove Book Club — 111

Follow Nichole — 112

More By Nichole Rose — 114

DEDICATION

For my favorite photographer, M.

About the Book

The heat between this curvy model and an infamous photographer will melt the camera. But will it lead to forever?

Trinity Larsen

I may own a modeling agency, but it's been a long time since I was in front of the camera.

Until I was named one of Le CRV Magazine's *Women of the Year*.

The infamous photographer, silver fox, and certified grump, Sage Grimes, is in charge of the photoshoot.

He makes me want to come alive for him...in more ways than one.

He asked for one night. I agreed.

But I think I made a mistake.

Because the night hasn't even ended, and I'm already hooked.

Sage Grimes

A photographer's role is to capture his subjects.

But we're not supposed to want to keep them for ourselves.

Except that's exactly what I want to do with Trinity Larsen.

I never expected to fall this hard and fast for that beautiful smile.

Asking for one night was a mistake.

Forever is where I should have started.

Because she's leaving in the morning, and I'm not ready to let her go.

Is it too late to change the rules of our agreement?

When this curvy model decides to give it up to a growly older man, she falls hard and fast for his bossy ways. Will one steamy night be the start of forever? If you enjoy steamy-sweet short reads, boss babes, and a little bit of risk, you'll love Trinity and Sage!

CHAPTER ONE
TRINITY

"I can't believe how incredible this place is," Mari Diego says, looking all around the ballroom of the hotel. Her dark hair and tattoos look stunning with her ballgown "It's gorgeous."

"Right?" Isabel Vargaz murmurs, sipping from her champagne flute. Her lipstick doesn't budge. Her makeup is on point tonight. Like Mari, she looks absolutely beautiful. "They really went all out for this. It's a little surreal."

"No kidding," I say, trying not to gape at our surroundings. Le CRV magazine outdid themselves for the Women of the Year party. The ballroom is absolutely breathtaking, as is the hotel itself. I feel a little like an imposter surrounded by so many amazing people. Everyone from NFL players to photographers to socialites turned out tonight to honor the five Women of the Year chosen by Le CRV.

Mari, Isabel, and I are three of the women being honored. Mari is a music producer and plus-size model. Isabel owns a mail-order specialty chocolate shop that is quickly becoming a force to be reckoned with. Two of the other nominees own fashion lines. I feel a little like the odd girl out. I'm just a former model turned-small-business-owner with a famous brother. Yet everyone has treated me like a queen since I arrived in New York.

It's a little crazy in the most amazing way possible.

"Trinity!"

I glance up from my champagne flute to see Vanna Arquette headed across the opulent ballroom toward me with Jimmy Catalano in tow. Her heels click on the tile floor, audible even over the murmur of fifteen different conversations happening all around me. Her red evening gown is absolutely gorgeous. It fits her curvy body like it was designed for her. It may very well have been.

Vanna is the Editor-in-Chief of Le CRV magazine, the biggest plus-size magazine in the United States. She started as a fashion columnist a decade ago but worked her way up. The magazine has exploded in popularity under her strict guidance. She works her ass off to make sure the magazine is the best it can be. Everyone who comes into contact with her seems to like her and the passion she brings to any project. I don't know her well, but nothing makes me happier than seeing another plus-size woman succeeding, especially in the world of high fashion.

Not too long ago, there weren't many of us. Unless you were a size zero, there were no seats at the table for you. That's changed in recent years. Thanks to the work of women like Vanna and Mari, the world is finally taking plus-size women seriously. People say I played a role in that too, but I think the credit really belongs to my brother, Gray. He's a professional hockey player. When I started modeling at eighteen, no one wanted to tell his little sister no.

People that normally would have slammed the door in my face or laughed at the thought of a plus-size model jumped to find me work. I went from working small, local jobs to appearing on magazine covers in the span of a few years. The work was grueling, and I had to fight to be heard every step of the way, but I'm glad I did it. I learned a lot about myself and the way the world works. I also quickly realized that I preferred the behind-the-scenes part more than the modeling parts.

I'm twenty-five now, and I own a plus-size modeling agency in California. My company is small, but our models have been featured in every major women's magazine in the world, including Le CRV. As for me, I haven't been in front of the camera in over three years.

I'm a little nervous about being in front of one again tomorrow, but Jimmy is a great photographer. I worked with him once about a year before I stopped modeling. We were doing a beach shoot for a new curvy swimwear line. It was one of the most stress-free jobs I've ever done. I don't hang onto many of the photos from my shoots, but I have a candid from that shoot hanging in my office. I love how it turned out. I'm staring out into the ocean with my hair all wild around my face and my arms around my knees. I think it's the first time anyone came close to capturing who I am underneath the makeup and poses.

I'm a little shy, and a bit of a homebody. At the end of the day, I love nothing more than stripping off my work clothes, putting on my pajamas, and drinking wine on the deck of my beach house while I read a good book or catch up with my family over FaceTime. I'm the exact opposite of this party, as beautiful as it is.

Don't get me wrong, I'm grateful to be here...but I'll be equally as grateful when I can respectfully sneak out to soak in the oversized tub in my hotel room. My Kindle has been calling my name all day. I fell asleep in the middle of a steamy scene last night. I'm dying to finish it!

It's not like I'll be getting to experience passion like that anytime soon. Truth be told, as glamorous as people think my life is...they're wrong. I've been on three dates in my entire life, and none of them went anywhere. Men think they want an independent woman until they're actually presented with one, and then they back away like they're afraid we bite.

It didn't bother me much until recently, but it's been weighing on me more and more of late. All of my friends are getting married and having babies. Even my brother has found his one, and I never thought he'd find his perfect match. He's awkward and nerdy and wildly inappropriate. But Camila is perfect for him.

She's my age and is as independent as I am. Women are always hitting on him because he's a hockey player, but Camila doesn't care about that. She genuinely cares about *him*, not his money and his fame. He worships the ground she walks on and would never ask her to make herself less or try to clip her wings.

Seeing how happy they are together really drove home how lonely my life has become. I've never seen him so damn *settled*. And she just glowed the entire time. I want that for myself. But I'm ready to give up on ever finding someone who not only loves me with his whole heart, but who accepts that my company is my baby.

I worked my ass off to make it what it is today. It's important to me, not just because I built it, but because of the men and women who sign with me. Modeling can be a vicious, toxic environment. I've seen far too many models being told they're too fat or too different or too *something* to make it.

I'm working to change that.

The men and women who sign with me have a voice, and the companies we work with are heavily vetted to ensure they respect our models as human beings. We don't work with brands who use plus-size models as examples of who not to be, or those who aren't size-inclusive. I want to live in a world where bodies of all shapes and sizes are celebrated, and that's what my company strives to create.

I won't give that up for anyone. It's too important to me.

Like my mom says, the right one wouldn't ever dream of asking me to do that anyway. He'd support me wholeheartedly and would want to see me and my company succeed.

But if the right one is out there...I wish he'd hurry up and find me because I'm not even sure who or what I'm supposed to be looking for at this point. Sometimes, I don't think anyone will ever check all my boxes. I want butterflies and weak knees and someone who knows how to be in control without trying to control me. I want romance and adventure and someone who can fuck me up against the wall with his hand around my throat and then tuck me in and cuddle me like in my books. Does that man even exist in real life?

If he does, I haven't met him yet.

"It looks like Vanna is on a mission," Isabel observes, smiling as Vanna and Jimmy dodge an elderly couple spinning around the dancefloor like they're eighteen again.

"She's always on a mission," Mari says, laughing. "She works harder than anyone I've ever met."

"Hey," I say when she and Jimmy finally reach us.

"I've been looking for you," Vanna says, pulling me into a hug before she greets Mari and Isabel with the same enthusiasm.

"I'm so sorry I wasn't here earlier in the week," I apologize to her once everyone has said their hellos. The other Women of the Year winners have already finished their photoshoots and everything. But there was no way I was going to miss Gray's wedding, even if it was a whirlwind. Thankfully, Vanna understands the importance of family. She rearranged everything to ensure I could be at Gray's wedding and still make my photoshoot. She's an angel.

"Family first," she says, pulling back to smile at me. "That brother of yours has caused quite a stir lately. It's nice to see things turning around for him."

"Thank you," I say. Gray had a little bit of embarrassing trouble with a charity contest and ended up being the punchline in a lot of late-night TV jokes. Meeting Camila turned things around for him, thankfully. "I'm really happy for him and Camila. She's going to be great for him."

I already love Camila. Her brother is a romance author, one of my favorites. We talked a little bit about the possibility of using some of my models on his covers. Not surprisingly, there's a shortage of plus-size cover models. Stock photography isn't flattering to plus-size women.

I'm excited to explore the possibilities with him and Camila.

"That's excellent news," Vanna says. "Please send my congratulations to both of them."

"I will," I promise, and then glance from her to Jimmy. "It's been a long time, stranger."

"And you've only gotten more beautiful," he says, winking at me, which makes Mari and Isabel both laugh. Jimmy is Italian American and can be quite charming. "I'm a little disappointed I won't get to shoot you this time, dear."

My brows furrow. "I thought you were running the shoot?"

"There was a slight change of plan," Vanna says. "Jimmy did the main shoot, but we decided to go a different direction with yours."

"Okay..." I say, not sure what she means or why Jimmy is smiling so widely.

Mari and Isabel don't seem to know what they're talking about either.

"Sage Grimes will be your photographer tomorrow," Vanna says.

"Sage Grimes?" I ask.

"Mmhmm," Jimmy says. "He seems quite smitten with you. He practically demanded that I step aside and let him run your photoshoot."

"Sage Grimes?" I say again...just to make sure we're talking about the same Sage Grimes. He's one of the best photographers in the world, and I'm not exaggerating. He's won every major photography award there is and had a number of photography scholarships named after him. He's literally that good. Every model in the business daydreams about making it big enough to merit a shoot with him. I'm *not* that well known. I've never even met him before!

Everyone says he's a complete grump. He doesn't tolerate bullshit well and has blackballed more than one model for diva-like behavior. No one tells Sage what to do. He can be demanding and bossy and will run a shoot however long it takes for him to get the perfect shot. There are a lot of rumors and stories about him, but I don't know how many are true or how many have simply grown with each retelling. He's an intensely private person, so no one really knows much about him. He lets his work speak for itself, and that's that.

Why in the world does he want to run my shoot?

"Mmhmm," Jimmy says again, his eyes twinkling with humor. "*The* Sage Grimes wants to do your cover shoot."

"Holy shit," Mari whispers.

Isabel blinks wide eyes at me. Unlike me, she's really outgoing, so I know if she's shocked into silence, this is a big deal. I really like her and Mari. I haven't known them long, but we've really bonded over sharing this experience. Good friends are hard to find as an adult!

"Wow," I whisper, blinking wide eyes at Vanna and Jimmy. My stomach flutters with nerves. I was never a big enough deal when I modeled to even dream about landing a Sage Grimes shoot. Wrapping my head around the fact that he's going to be the photographer tomorrow is hard enough. Knowing that he asked to photograph me is...wow. "Is he sure he has the right person?"

"Positive," Vanna says. "He's done a few pieces for us before. When he asked to do this one, we jumped at the chance. It's a fantastic way to bring attention not just to your shoot, but to all of the Women of the Year nominees and the incredible things you're doing for plus-size women." She meets my gaze. "If you're not comfortable with the change, I'm prepared to tell him no."

This is what I love about working with Vanna. She's not just a great editor, she's a great person and a fantastic advocate for women. There are horror stories about the editors of other magazines, but you only ever hear positive things about Le CRV. They genuinely care about plus-size women, not as a commodity but as people.

Body positivity and advocacy isn't just a band-wagon for Le CRV. It's a way of life. The magazine is so popular because it doesn't focus on celebrities who already have a platform, but on celebrating the achievements, success, and daily life of everyday women. They work hard to make sure the women they highlight are comfortable and are part of the process.

If I tell her that I don't want to work with Sage, I have no doubt that she'll tell him no, even if it means losing him as a photographer in the future. For a second, I consider saying no, simply because I can't fathom why someone with a reputation like his would want to photograph someone like me—a business owner who hasn't been in front of a camera in years. But rabid curiosity silences me.

I want to know why he wants to photograph me. And I want to meet him. I've heard so many things about him over the years, but I've never even been in the same room with him. I'm damn curious to see if he lives up to all of the hype. Besides, even if meeting him is a little intimidating, adaptability is the name of the game in this industry. Last-minute changes are to be expected. Anyone who wants to make it in the fashion industry knows this. I would never want to risk harming Le CRV's reputation or the reputation of my agency simply because I was too nervous to work with Sage.

"The change is fine," I promise Vanna and Jimmy, much to their relief.

"We were going to fight if you said no," Isabel says, teasing me.

Mari laughs quietly and then bobs her head in agreement, which makes all of us laugh. Only a crazy person would say no to Sage Grimes.

"I'm so excited for you," Vanna says, beaming at me. "I can't wait to see the pure gold he's able to get with you. I just know it's going to be fantastic!"

I gulp and then immediately blush, praying neither of them noticed. The more we talk about Sage, the more nervous I become...and I was already nervous enough about being in front of the camera again. But I can do this. If letting him run this photoshoot brings attention to the men and women I represent, I'll be the best damn model he's ever worked with.

CHAPTER TWO
SAGE

"What's taking so long?" I growl to myself, pacing back and forth across the rooftop while I wait for Trinity Larsen to make her appearance. She's been in hair and makeup for the last hour, which is ridiculous if you ask me. She doesn't need any of that shit to be beautiful. It just detracts from what she has naturally.

I wanted to rush in there and take charge as soon as Gabby let me know she was here, but I talked myself out of it. I've been looking forward to this day since I found out Trinity was one of the nominees being honored by Le CRV. My niece, Georgia, is one of her models. She's been talking about Trinity nonstop for the last six months. It piqued my curiosity, so I looked her up.

I'm not sure what I was expecting, but it wasn't the goddess staring back at me from my screen. As soon as I saw her, I knew I'd do whatever I had to do to get her in front of my camera. I've photographed a lot of beautiful women in my life, but none of them ever got to me like a single image of Trinity did. The photograph was amateurish at best, but when you have a subject like Trinity, it doesn't matter who's behind the camera. She's stunning, sexy without even trying.

There's an artless innocence about her that's rare in this world. Everything from hair to breasts to waists are surgically enhanced these days, but there's nothing fake about her. Those plump lips and gray eyes are real, so are her high cheekbones and sooty lashes. She's tall and curvy with thick thighs and an ass I can't stop thinking about. She'd probably slap me if she knew how many times I've fantasized about burying my face between those cheeks and eating her until she's screaming for mercy.

I'm not sure I'd have any to offer her.

My dick has been hard for the last month straight. That's not normal for me.

I haven't been a saint in my life, but I'm not someone who sleeps around either. A lot of photographers jump into bed with their models. I don't. Women aren't objects. I refuse to play the bullshit game so many photographers play with them. They treat it like a competition amongst themselves, keeping score of who they've fucked and comparing notes. That's not how I operate. I've worked too hard to get where I am to risk it for a quick lay.

Since MeToo, a lot of photographers have been sweating bullets, worried they'd be the next one called out for their gross, predatory behavior. I have no sympathy for them. Like I've said a thousand times, they wouldn't be worried if they weren't guilty. I'm not worried.

I may be an asshole, but I don't prey on models or sleep around. At forty-four, I'm too goddamn old for games, and a long string of one-night stands never interested me. It's been a decade since my dick was in anything but my own hand.

I've been married to my job for most of my life. But I've never wanted anything the way I want Trinity Larsen. It's not just that she's stunning either. She's smart as hell. Not many people find success at such an early age, nor do they use it to advocate for inclusivity the way she does. The men and women who sign with her have a little mama bear in their corner, one willing to go to war to ensure they're treated with respect and dignity.

That's a rarity. Getting ahead is the name of the game, and other people are often collateral damage. Especially plus-size models. How many have signed on to model, only to become a cautionary tale sold to the public? For decades, curvy women have been posed with junk food or exercise equipment in their hands while the fashion industry sold the narrative that big is antithetical to beautiful.

It's a crock of shit. Some of the most gorgeous people I've photographed have been big, beautiful women like Trinity. I desperately want to photograph her. Even if she tells me to fuck off, I want to be the one capturing every flicker of emotion across her face, every beautiful smile. She's a goddamn dream shoot for me, one of those rare beauties who look incredible from every angle, in every light. But no one has truly captured her yet. She looks like a goddess in every photograph, but they aren't her.

It took me all of five seconds to recognize it. The face the world sees is a mask. The most interesting parts of her are tucked away behind those pretty eyes and flirty smiles. I'm dying to know who she is when the world isn't watching. Is she the strong businesswoman? The confident model? The reserved young woman? The artless seductress? Everything I've learned about her suggests she's a little bit of all of the above.

Like me, she doesn't seem to date. Her business and her family are her life. She cares so much for both...but who is taking care of her? Who holds her when she's sad or carries her to bed when she falls asleep on the couch? I want it to be me.

Getting Vanna and Jimmy Catalano to agree to let me do this shoot took a little work, but Vanna called last night to let me know that Trinity agreed. I don't think I slept at all. I was too goddamn impatient. I'm also worried as fuck.

I'm not exactly someone that's well-liked. Respected, yes. Damn good at my job, yes. But liked? Not particularly. People call me an asshole because I know what I want and don't put up with bullshit. I've been making my own rules for most of my life. I've pissed off more than a person or two along the way. They say I'm demanding, blunt, and that I expect perfection. They're not wrong. But those traits are what got me where I am. People know my name. They've seen my photographs in every major magazine or hanging in galleries. I've traveled the world and seen everything there is to see.

I never cared what anyone thought before now. I care about this one. There's something about her I can't shake.

My life is lonely. It never bothered me until I saw her picture and realized she's what has always been missing. I want to show this woman the world and watch her conquer it. I want to be the man who stands at her side while she moves mountains, the one who knows every thought in her head. I want to be the man who fucks her raw and then puts her in a bubble bath.

Am I crazy? Quite possibly. Will it stop me? No.

I've tried to quit thinking about her. I told myself to get a grip and let it go a thousand times since I looked her up a month ago. Five minutes later, she'd be on my mind again. It pissed me off at a first because I didn't understand it. I still don't. But I'm done fighting it.

I came here to make Trinity mine. I'm not leaving without giving it my best effort.

The roof access door swings open behind me. I spin on my heel, expecting to see Gabby. I told her to let me know when Trinity was ready. Instead, my gaze lands on Trinity. As soon as I see her, my mind goes blank.

She's even more beautiful in person. Her hair is tousled, her makeup natural. Her outfit is a one-piece black swimsuit, a thin sarong, and a floppy hat, which she's holding in her hands. Vanna said one of the other nominees designed the swimwear. The thin white robe Trinity's wearing over it doesn't offer much protection. Every curve and dip of her body is on display. I have to keep from reaching for my dick to readjust as he lengthens in my pants.

Her gray eyes run over me, and her teeth sink into her bottom lip. I hope like hell she likes what she sees. Like most men my age, my body isn't what it used to be. I work-out and run every day, but I'm not ripped. I'm thick everywhere, sturdy, with a barrel chest and skin that's seen more than its fair share of time under the sun. My hair was silver long before it was popular. It's also a little shaggy. Compared to her, I'm an old bastard.

"Sage Grimes?" she says, her voice soft and sweet, lilting.

"That's me," I growl, striding across the rooftop toward her.

She shivers a little like she's cold.

"Get her a blanket," I growl at my assistant, who is hovering behind her in the stairway. "It's too fucking cold up here for her to be this uncovered between setups."

Gabby jumps to obey, murmuring an apology beneath her breath. After half a dozen years, she's used to my abrupt nature. She gives me shit about it more often than not. So does her wife.

"I'm fine, really," Trinity says, stepping out onto the roof. The sun hits her, turning her hair into a halo of gold. It's not all one color like I thought, but varying shades of blonde, red, and light brown. Her gray eyes dance over me, heating me more than the sun beating down on me. "I'm Trinity Larsen."

One dainty hand dangles in the air, waiting for me to reach for it. I hesitate for a split second, slightly worried I'll cross a line and pull her into my arms if I touch her. But when her brows furrow and a hint of anxiety enters her gaze, I grasp onto her like a lifeline.

As soon as our hands connect, an electric surge rolls through me. I don't have to ask to know she feels it too. She jumps a foot into the air, her pupils dilating.

"W-what was that?" she asks.

Ah, baby. You haven't felt anything yet. Wait until I'm inside you, grinding against that sweet little clit.

"It's nice to meet you, Miss Larsen," I murmur, tugging her a tiny bit closer. She smells sweet, like peaches and sugar. There's a faint note beneath, one I can't place. Whatever it is has my stomach growling and my mouth watering. "I've heard a lot about you."

"From who?"

I smile as soon as the question erupts from her lips, rampant curiosity in her gaze. She knows I asked for this shoot. She wants to know why but is too polite to ask outright. "My niece is one of your models."

She shivers again and I realize she was telling the truth earlier. She isn't cold. She likes my voice. Every time I speak, her gaze drifts to my lips and her eyes get a little glassy. Huh. Sounds turn her on. My voice is gruff, gravely. I don't normally say much, but I'll talk as long as she likes if it makes her happy.

"Who is your niece?"

"Georgia."

Her expression softens, recognition immediately firing in her eyes. "Georgia Dillard is your niece?"

"Mmhmm."

"I didn't know that," she says, smiling at me with genuine warmth.

"I know." I tug her another step closer to me. We're sharing the same bubble, but she doesn't seem to notice how close we're standing. Hell, she doesn't seem to realize I'm still holding her hand either. All of her attention is on me. Her gaze dances up and down like she isn't sure where she wants to focus. She's tall, but I'm a big guy. She barely reaches my shoulder.

"Did she ask you to do this?" she asks, those teeth leaving indentions in her pouty bottom lip.

"No," I growl, my zipper leaving imprints on my dick when I glance down and see the swells of her breasts. Her skin is porcelain, almost translucent. I can't wait to put my mouth all over her.

Not yet, I remind myself. *Business first, old man. Watch yourself.*

"Oh." The corners of her lips turn down into a frown. I instantly hate seeing it. She should only ever smile. When she's mine, I'll make sure that's all she ever does. She was made to be spoiled, adored. I can't wait to be the one who gets to do that for her.

"You're stunning, baby girl," I say, unable to resist. "I wanted to photograph you as soon as I saw you."

"You saw me?"

"Pictures," I growl, not elaborating. I don't want to freak her out, and I'm pretty sure telling her I've been jacking my cock to images of her for the last month straight is liable to do exactly that. She doesn't know me from Adam. I don't want her thinking hitting on my models is something I do often because it's not. If she were anyone else, this conversation would be going a lot different than it is right now. "Are you ready to get started?"

She blinks those sooty lashes, seemingly startled, as if she forgot why we're here. And then anxiety flashes in her gaze again. "I think so," she says, and then grimaces. "Can I tell you something?"

"Anything."

"I haven't been in front of the camera in a while."

"How long?"

"Three years. I decided I liked the business side of things better than the modeling side of things." A self-conscious laugh burbles from her lips. "I'm afraid you may be disappointed."

"Hey." I take a risk and reach out to tip her chin up until her eyes meet mine again. "You could never be a disappointment, Trinity. Trust me?"

"I..." She stares at me for a moment, her lips parted and a soft look in her eyes. Her expression darkens, heating. Her face flushes, but it's not from embarrassment. The tip of her tongue peeks from between her lips and then she nods. "Yes."

CHAPTER THREE
TRINITY

"You're from Los Angeles?" Sage asks. "Turn to the left."

"I live in Los Angeles," I respond, turning like he instructed. Once I'm where he wants me, he grunts, letting me know I'm where he wants me. "But I was born and raised in Nashville."

"Nice city. Lift your arm over your head," he growls, rapidly snapping photos.

I fight the urge to shiver as his gruff voice rolls over me and then do as instructed. I lift my arm, letting my fingers graze the back of my head. My lips are slightly parted, my eyes locked on Sage as he moves around in front of me, trying to get the best angle.

"You live with a boyfriend?" he growls, lowering the camera until we make eye contact over the top of it. His expression is intense, fiery. God, he's beautiful. And the way he keeps looking at me makes me feel beautiful too.

"No," I say, holding his gaze. "No boyfriends."

"Good girl."

I shiver as that deep purr rolls over me.

He notices. One corner of his mouth tics upward into a rusty smile. His gaze rolls over me again, setting my blood on fire in my veins. And then he raises the camera again, effectively breaking eye contact with me. I take the opportunity to look him up and down again before the shutter starts clicking.

I've heard so much about him over the years, but no one ever mentioned that he's sexy as sin. He's thick everywhere, like the redwood giants in California. His arms are as big around as tree trunks, his skin golden-brown from the sun. Despite my size, he dwarves me in a way I find all too appealing. Keeping my eyes off him is impossible.

His eyes remind me of seafoam. They're so full of intensity and command that I find myself obeying his instructions without thought. He speaks and my body just reacts on instinct. I think his voice is partially responsible for that. It's deep and dark, as full of command as those gorgeous eyes. As soon as I heard it the first time, my panties grew damp.

His silver hair is a little on the longer side. I keep imagining clutching it while he has his face between my thighs, tickling me with that silver beard. It's hard to focus when X-rated images of this man keep popping into my mind every five seconds. But he's so damn attractive it's ridiculous. No one warned me that I'd want to melt into a puddle at his feet every time he growled at me. Or that his rusty smile would make my knees tremble.

Every time he murmurs, "Good girl", I have to bite my tongue to keep from whimpering out loud. I'm so turned on it's ridiculous. I can't remember the last time that happened. Actually, I can. It's never happened. Ever. No one ever makes me weak in the knees, and I've never been so eager to please anyone before in my life.

"What about you?" I ask.

"Boyfriends?" I hear the amusement in his voice.

"Or girlfriends."

"Neither," he growls. "Never had time for a woman." He hesitates for a second, his finger hovering just above the button on his camera. "That'll be changing now."

I open my mouth to ask why and then snap it closed again, worried about how he might answer that question. If he says he found someone, I might actually cry, which makes no sense to me. I just met him a few hours ago! And yet...as soon as he touched me, I felt like the world shifted beneath my feet. I know he felt it too. I saw it in his eyes.

"Turn the light to the right," he orders his assistant.

I forgot she was even here. All I've been able to see is Sage. He's the sun, blotting out everything else. I don't think it's his reputation either. It's him. He's so damn *big*. I've spent seven years of my life with male models. Not one of them ever set my body on fire like this man does. There's nothing soft about him. He's rough and hard. I understand why people are intimidated by him. Some people are born with presence. It's impossible to overlook them. He's one of those people. He carries himself like he's used to being obeyed without question.

I shift my foot forward, cocking my hip back and turning my head slightly. He snaps several more photos while Gabby plays with the lighting, trying to get it just right. The sun drifted behind clouds a few minutes ago and it's getting chilly on the roof. We're only ten stories up, but the East River is just a stone's throw away and it's windy. It feels like we're in our own little world beside the iconic rooftop pool.

My mind drifts from the shoot right back to the man behind the camera. Is it just my imagination, or is he into me too? I think he is. He keeps looking at me like he wants to eat me for dinner. I definitely want to have *him* for dinner.

Another explicit images pops into my mind, causing me to stumble. This time, he's got his hands tangled in my hair, thrusting into my mouth. His eyes are on fire, his lip caught between his teeth. Mine are stretched wide around him in silent bliss.

Good God. I'm going to hell.

"Right there," Sage says. "Don't move, baby girl."

I freeze exactly where I am, holding the accidental pose. He keeps calling me that. I never imagined such a simple pet name could sound so sexy. But I love the way he says it. Hell, who am I kidding? I've known him for a matter of hours and there's nothing about him I don't like.

He snaps several more photos and then lowers his camera.

I stay in position, waiting for his cue that I'm free to move around.

His eyes come to me, one corner of his lip lifting. "Vanna will love these," he says, holding out a hand to me. "Come here and look."

I obediently cross the rooftop on bare feet to stand next to him. He wraps his hand around my wrist, tugging me closer to him. The heat of his body sears into me. He's burning hot, a veritable inferno. I catch myself swaying toward him and lock my knees to keep from pressing up against his body.

He holds the camera up, allowing me to see the photos he just took.

"Oh, wow," I whisper, staring at the small screen. The pool is at my feet with the city at my back. My expression is heated, my lips slightly parted. I look like I just had sex or want to have sex. I'm not sure. But the pictures are good. "I look..."

"You look sexy as hell," Sage murmurs, turning his head to look at me.

"Thank you," I whisper, my cheeks heating at the compliment.

"What were you thinking about?"

You thrusting between my lips.

"N-nothing," I lie.

"Nothing?"

I shake my head.

"Liar," he whispers, moving his face closer to me so Gabby can't hear what he says. "You whimpered right before I took this photo, Trinity."

Oh my god.

"I didn't," I gasp quietly.

"You did." His warm breath hits my neck, his beard tickling my skin. "You were thinking naughty thoughts. Were they about me, sweet lamb?"

"N...no."

"Liar," he says again, his voice a gruff purr that liquefies my insides. "But that's all right. You'll tell me what you were thinking about before the day is over." It might be my imagination, but I think I feel his tongue caress the shell of my ear before he takes a step away from me and calls for Gabby.

I stand right where I'm at, my mind spinning. Part of me is horrified that he heard me whimper and knows I was thinking about things I shouldn't. But a small part—one I never even knew existed until today—trembles in excitement that he knows. That part wants him to know I was thinking dirty thoughts about him. It wants him thinking them about me too.

Lord, have mercy. This could be bad. The last thing I need is for someone like Sage to tell the world that I spent the shoot flirting with him or acting inappropriately. No one wants to work with someone who is considered difficult or unprofessional. I may not model anymore, but I have a whole company of people to consider. They count on me to be able to book them jobs. If Sage blackballs me, he blackballs my models too.

I have to get it together and get through this shoot.

Sage and Gabby talk back and forth for a few minutes before Sage murmurs something and then glances at me. Gabby nods and then moves away from Sage. A couple seconds later, she starts cleaning up.

"Are we finished?" I ask, surprised.

"No." Sage strolls back toward me. He walks like a wild animal stalking its prey. His footfalls are steady, solid, but soundless. I fight the urge to shiver as his gaze sweeps down my body and then back up. "But it's getting too cold out here for you. We're moving indoors for the rest of the shoot."

"Oh."

"Is that okay with you?"

I nod my agreement as he snags my robe from the back of a lounger where I left it.

"Thank you," I murmur, shrugging into it when he holds it out to me.

"Are you comfortable with this being just the two of us?" he asks. "It looks like it's going to rain soon, and I'd rather not leave the equipment out here."

I glance at the sky and then over at Gabby, who is taking down the lights. My stomach turns a somersault at the thought of being alone with Sage. He's already got me all twisted into knots and turned upside down. But I don't want him to risk his equipment. It's not cheap.

"That's fine," I say, praying I can keep it together long enough to get through the rest of this shoot without embarrassing myself.

"Relax," Sage says an hour later, stalking around the hotel room like a caged lion.

I inhale a deep breath and then slowly exhale, trying to follow that command. It's impossible though. There's a bed right behind him, and I can't seem to forget that long enough to relax into the pose. Every time I think I've got it under control, he shifts slightly, and the bed comes blazing back into focus.

My stomach flips and my nerves start clamoring all over again every single time.

"Turn to the left," he says. As soon as I move, he sighs. "Left, baby girl. Not right."

"Sorry," I whisper, my face flaming. I quickly move to the left, only to list sideways. Reaching out, I grab the back of the chaise just before I land on my ass in the floor.

"Shit," Sage says, lowering the camera. "Are you okay?"

"Yes," I whisper and then exhale a breath. This has turned into a train wreck. He probably thinks I'm a complete disaster. "I'm sorry."

"Stop apologizing."

"Sor..."

He stalks across the room toward me, a deep groove in his forehead from him frowning so hard. "Am I making you uncomfortable, Trinity?"

"No, I..." I trail off with a shake of my head. "No."

He eyes me for a minute, his lips pursed. "You're nervous. Why?"

"I haven't modeled in a long time," I remind him. "I'm just rusty."

He cocks a brow at me, clearly not buying my excuse. "Bullshit. You could be out of the game for half a century and still be a natural. You move like a dream," he says. "Being alone with me makes you nervous."

"I–"

"I'm just not sure if it's because I make you uncomfortable or if it's because you're attracted to me," he murmurs before I can utter a denial. "If it's the former, I'll get Gabby in here so you're able to relax. I don't want you feeling anxious around me."

I inhale a deep breath, reaching for a little courage. "And if it's the latter?"

"And if it's the latter," he says, squatting down beside the chaise so we're eye level, "I'll tell you that you aren't the only one, we'll finish this shoot, and then I'll ask you out to dinner." He holds up a hand, halting me before I can respond. "But I promised myself to behave during this shoot, so I'm trying like hell to honor that promise."

"Oh," I whisper, disappointment flowing through me. The way he says it makes me think he's done this before. I don't like the way that feels. It's like a thorn stabbing me right through the heart. I've never felt this way before, and I guess I just expected that he hadn't ever felt it before either. But who am I kidding? He's older, gorgeous, and spends his days with some of the most beautiful women on the planet. He's probably been with a million women.

"What's that look?" he demands, reaching out to turn my face toward him. He's scowling, his eyes narrowed like he wants to fight whatever upset me. Which is honestly kind of sweet but only makes me feel like an even bigger dork.

"Nothing," I say, shaking my head. "Nothing. I'm just being crazy. Let's just finish this."

"No."

"No?" I blink at him.

"Not until you tell me what you were just thinking about," he says.

"It was nothing," I say, willing him to believe it.

He holds my gaze, silently commanding me to tell him. I try to resist, really, I do. But it's virtually impossible when he's so close I can smell his intoxicating scent and see the flecks of gold in his eyes. When I feel the heat of his big body calling to me. Everything about him makes me want to obey, just to make him call me a good girl again.

Why is that so sexy to me?

"I am nervous about being alone with you," I blurt out.

It might be my imagination, but for a split second, distress flashes through his expression. And then he blinks it away, his gaze settling on my face. He goes completely still, barely even seeming to breathe. "Why does being along with me make you nervous?"

"I don't want to mess this up," I say, not sure how to explain without sounding like a crazy person. "You're not just a photographer, Sage. You're pretty much the best photographer in the world. I don't want to do something wrong when it could impact my models or my business. I don't want you to think I'm not professional."

His brows furrow, his expression darkening.

Uh oh.

"You think I'd do something to hurt your business?"

"Not exactly..."

"Explain," he growls.

I don't understand how he's even hotter when he's angry. It's really not fair.

"I just..." I huff out a breath and send up a silent prayer that I don't live to regret being honest with him. "I'm ridiculously attracted to you, and you know I was thinking about dirty things outside. Now we're alone and I'm freaking out because there's a bed right behind you and I'm still thinking dirty things about you," I say all at once and then slap a hand over my mouth. "Please don't blackball me."

"Blackball you?" He blinks at me, genuinely shocked. "You think I'm going to be pissed that you're attracted to me, Trinity?"

I bob my head in a nod.

"I'd never do anything to hurt you," he vows, his voice so somber I don't doubt him. His eyes blaze like the sun, that same vow reflecting deep in their depths. "Would you believe I've been worried about roughly the same thing?"

"You have?" I ask, trying to wrap my head around that. He's so...*him*. Gorgeous. Talented. Older. There's no way he's been worried about being alone with me. Except I know he isn't lying. I'd stake my life on the fact that he's being honest with me right now.

"You think I go around making demands to work with certain people often?" he asks, cocking a brow at me.

"I guess I assumed you..." I trail off, not honestly sure if I thought that or not.

He cocks a brow at me. "You think all my models get my dick hard? Or that the thought of getting time alone with them makes me fucking crazy? You're wrong." He reaches out slowly, carefully, as if giving me time to move away from him. I don't though. I stay right where I am. His rough fingers touch the side of my face, turning it toward him. "I don't fuck my models, Trinity."

My stomach sinks, despair bubbling up hard and fast.

"You'll be the first."

"I...what?" I ask, not sure I heard him correctly. Praying I did. So turned on, I'm shaking.

"You'll be the first model I've ever taken to bed," he says, speaking slowly, succinctly. "You're the first one I've ever wanted to fuck. And I want it so goddamn badly, I should be ashamed of myself. That little slip of fabric standing between me and your sweet little cunt has been taunting me all fucking day, daring me to slip it to the side and bury my face between your legs. I didn't care if we were on the roof or if Gabby was standing right there. I thought about it all morning."

No one ever talks to me this way, so bluntly. But he's not like anyone I know. He's Sage freaking Grimes. He could have anyone he wanted, yet I'm the one he wanted to photograph. I'm the one he keeps staring at like he can't look away. I'm the one he wants to...fuck.

Oh my goodness.

This is really happening, isn't it?

"Give me one night, lamb," he murmurs, stroking those long fingers along the side of my face. "Let me take you out and show you off the way you deserve. Let me make love to you, show you how good it can be between us. You won't regret it."

I'm pretty sure he's wrong about that. I already know one night won't be enough for me. He's barely even touched me, and my body already craves him. I'm pretty sure if I get any closer to him, I'll become addicted. And when the night ends, it'll break my heart.

But I don't tell him no.

I want this. I want him. Even if it's only for a night.

"One night?" I ask.

Something flashes in his eyes too quickly for me to read. He blinks it away and nods. "One night," he growls. "Say yes."

"Yes."

CHAPTER FOUR
SAGE

Trinity Larsen is trying to kill me, I'm certain of it. She writhes around on the chaise, pouting at the camera...turning my dick to steel. Every shot is better than the last. She's a little temptress, her confidence unshakable now that she's not worried about fucking up or being deemed unprofessional for wanting me. I've never been more turned on, or more satisfied in my life.

I already know these photos won't be going to Le CRV. I don't want anyone seeing her like this. She's on fire, burning hot enough to melt the lens of my camera. Keeping my hands to myself is taking every ounce of self-control I possess. Sweat trickles between my shoulder blades as I stalk around her, capturing every move she makes.

This is the Trinity I wanted to capture, the woman she is underneath. My girl is equal parts shy little lamb and wicked temptress. Both are evident in every move she makes. She rolls to her stomach, lifting her ass into the air. A playful smile dances across her lips as she tosses her head back. Her cheeks are flushed, the pulse in her throat thrumming. I don't think she even realizes how fucking beautiful she is right now. Or how close to breaking I am.

Neither of us has spoken for the last hour. I don't need to direct her. She's in charge here. I'm just capturing what she gives me. She really is a natural at this. I'm not going to lie though... I'm a little relieved she prefers the business side of things. Sharing her with the world is less and less appealing every time I look at her. I've never been greedy, but I want to keep this woman all to myself.

One day, she's going to pose nude for me. No one else will ever see those photos either. They'll be my personal collection, for my eyes only. I'll cover the walls of my bedroom in them, so everywhere I look, I see her. Her full breasts and round ass. The pale skin of her thighs. The deep curve of her waist. That seductive smile.

Why the fuck did I ask for one night? It's not nearly long enough. I want forever.

If I can't convince her that she wants the same by the time morning comes, I'm fucked. She's flying back to Los Angeles tomorrow, where she'll be surrounded by men who can give her the world. That's a problem for me because she had my heart in her hands before I ever met her. Her sweet fumbling earlier only confirmed that it was hers. She was so damn worried I'd be upset that she was thinking dirty shit about me, completely clueless that I've been hard all day, trying like hell not to make her uncomfortable or cross a line.

That ship sailed as soon as she confirmed that she feels the same way. She's mine now. Before she leaves this room tomorrow, she'll be wearing my marks in her skin, dripping my cum from her little holes. I'll do whatever I have to do to convince her that this isn't a one-night type of deal.

"Enough," I rasp, unable to take anymore when she arches her back, putting that round ass high in the air. I toss the camera onto the bed, equal parts turned on and frustrated. "You're trying to break me, aren't you?"

"No." She bites her lip and then giggles a little. "Maybe."

I growl at her, which makes her laugh again. That sound is already my favorite. It's so damn innocent and refreshing. How she's survived in this world for so long without losing that artlessness, I don't know. But I want to drop to my knees and thank God for it. There's nothing hardened or cynical about her. She isn't jaded or spoiled. She's the sweetest little lamb.

I stalk toward her across the room, practically panting from exertion.

She rolls onto her back, her long hair spilling over the side of the chaise. It's so long it nearly sweeps the floor. She's a dirty version of Rapunzel locked up tight in her tower. Only I'm not a prince, and I'm not climbing her hair to reach her. I'll have that wrapped around my fist while I'm fucking her from behind.

"Did you get any good shots?" she asks.

I grunt in response, drawing to a stop beside her. From this vantage point, I can see the line of freckles scattered across the bridge of her nose. I can also see the way her body trembles faintly and she rubs her thighs together, searching for friction to ease the ache between them. Teasing me made her horny.

"Come here and I'll show you," I say, holding out a hand to her.

She hesitates for a split second before taking my hand and allowing me to pull her up from the chaise. Her warm body collides with mine, soft meeting hard, yielding to it.

"You enjoy teasing me," I say, plunging my hand into her hair to tip her head back until she's staring up at me. She moans quietly, though I'm not sure if it's because she enjoys the submissive position or if it's because she enjoys teasing me. Both, maybe.

"Yes," she says, her gaze flitting across my face. She isn't nervous now. In fact, she looks entirely too pleased with herself. She likes knowing she can rile me up, get me heated. That's all right. Just so long as she knows she'll be paying for it. Whenever she's feeling like a little minx, I'll let her play. She can torture me all she wants. Because when she's done, it's my turn. Only, I won't tease her from across the room. When she breaks for me, it'll be with me all over her.

"You ready to pay the price, lamb?" I ask, tugging her head back further. My free hand skims down her back and onto her ass. I squeeze one plump cheek in my hand, earning another soft moan from her.

"What..." She licks her lips. "What's the price?"

"A kiss."

"Just one?" Her hands settle on my shoulders, slide down, and then back up as she feels the muscles bunch beneath her palms. Her pupils dilate, letting me know she likes my body. Thank God for that. Unlike her, I'm not soft or sweet or beautiful. I'm not a model, and my body is far from perfect. But it'll bring her more pleasure than she'll be able to handle. I'll make sure of that.

"To start," I murmur, dipping my head until our lips are a breath apart. I hover there, waiting for her to take it further, to kiss me. I don't want her feeling like she has no say here. If this isn't what she wants, I won't push her. I won't be one of those shady motherfuckers who takes what isn't willingly given. She has the power here, and I want her to know that. "You can tell me no."

"I know," she whispers, leaning forward. "But I don't want to tell you no, Sage." Her mouth brushes mine. Her lips are soft, her breath warm and sweet.

I growl like a starving animal, my entire body vibrating with the sound. I take control then, flicking my tongue against the seam of her lips until she opens for me. As soon as she does, I plunge my tongue into her mouth, demanding more. I want everything she has, want to possess every part of her. She moans when I slide my tongue against hers, stroking it.

Her hands dig into my shoulder as she breathes a whimper into my mouth. I steal it from her, taking it deep into my lungs and holding it there. My hand in her hair tightens, angling her head so I can get deeper, kiss her harder. An inferno rages to life between us, powerful and bright. She feels it too. She whines my name, wrapping her body around me.

I boost her up into my arms, growling when her legs wrap around my waist. My hands skim over her ass, squeezing, kneading, grinding her little clit against the bulge in my jeans. Rationally, I know I need to slow this down, but no part of me wants to do that. I want all of her here and now. More than I've ever wanted anything, I want this woman bare beneath me, begging me not to stop.

"Sage," she whimpers. "Oh my god."

"You like that, Trinity?" I bounce her up and down, tilting my pelvis so my dick hits her clit each time I move. She turns to putty in my hands, melting into me, mewling into my mouth.

Fuck, she's a hot little thing, so fucking sexy. She doesn't even have to try. It's just who she is.

"Yes! Don't stop." Her head lolls on her neck, making it impossible for me to keep kissing her. That's fine though. I run my mouth down her throat and onto her chest, kissing all over the swells of her breasts.

She gasps when my beard tickles her delicate skin.

"It'll feel even better against your thighs when I'm eating you, baby girl," I growl against her skin.

"I know," she says, and then shocks the shit out of me. "That—oh my God, that feels so good—that's what I was thinking about on the roof."

"Shit," I growl, a spurt of cum soaking my boxers.

"I thought about having you in my mouth too."

"Trinity." I'm not sure if I'm asking her to stop talking or begging her to continue. If she wants me in her mouth, I'll give it to her. But not before I get mine on her and eat that little cunt until she's screaming the roof down around us.

It's a good thing they put us on the top floor for this shoot. I don't want anyone to hear what I'm going to do to her in this room. The filthy things I'll say to her...and the sounds she'll make. Those are for us alone. No one else.

I slip my hands beneath the band of her bathing suit, grasping her bare ass in my palms. Her skin is soft everywhere. There are little dimples in her flesh that make my dick even harder, as impossible as that is. She's young, but there's nothing girlish about her.

Most models are consumed with looking good for the camera. They starve themselves just to make it. It's not their fault. That's what's expected of them. As soon as they gain a pound or two, they're told they're too fat and are tossed aside for someone younger, someone smaller. They sacrifice their health for their jobs, and no one bats a lash. That's not Trinity. She's all woman, with a woman's body. She has stretch marks on her thighs and dimples on her ass. Her belly is round, her thighs thick. She has no idea how fucking sexy I find that.

I grind her against my dick, snarling against her chest when her thighs quiver around my hips. She's so turned on, she's already on the verge of coming all over me. I want her to do it.

"Soak that little bathing suit for me, Trinity," I growl. "You've been hurting for it all day, haven't you?"

"Yes," she gasps, her nails scrabbling down my back. She digs her heels into my ass, using it as leverage to work herself up and down as she chases the pleasure.

I pull the top of her suit down with my teeth, freeing one fat nipple. And Jesus. I can't wait to get her naked and see every inch of her. Her nipple is a hard little pebble, more brown than pink. It's fucking perfect.

I pull it into my mouth, wrapping my tongue around it. It taste like peaches, just like the rest of her. I bite down, pulling it through my teeth. She cries out in shock, my name leaving her lips in a sharp cry of disbelief.

As soon as I hear it, what little control I have left shatters. She bounces on the bed when she lands, knocking the camera off onto the floor. I don't even spare it a second thought as I all but launch myself onto the bed with her. Before she can even cry out, I'm on top of her, dry humping her like my fucking life depends on it.

"You're a virgin," I growl, yanking the top of her bathing suit down to free her other breast. As soon as it pops free, I've got my mouth on it, sucking her nipple into my mouth, trying to consume her alive.

Never in my life have I felt like I do right now. Hearing that sound, realizing she's never done this before...that I'm the man she's trusting with this piece of her...my entire fucking *world* just shifted. My girl needs someone to guide her, to teach her.

And she chose me. I'm the lucky motherfucker she decided to share this with.

"Sage," she says, trembling and shaking beneath me, suddenly nervous. "Sage, I...I..."

"Don't lie to me," I growl, lifting my head until our eyes meet. I see the worry in hers, the anxiety. She's afraid I'll change my mind, decide I don't want this. Fuck that. That cherry is mine, just like the rest of her. "You've never done this before, have you, lamb?"

"I..." She trails off and shakes her head, her eyes wide.

"Good girl," I murmur, kissing all over her chest, rewarding her for her honesty. "You want me to be your first, Trinity?"

She doesn't hesitate this time. "Yes. Please, Sage. I need you," she says, wrapping her legs around my hips like she's afraid I'll pull away or leave her aching. That won't ever happen though. She doesn't know it yet, but once I'm in her, I plan to be the only man to ever know her like this. I'll be her first, her last, her only.

I don't tell her that though. Not yet. Because I'm a little worried I'll spook her and send her running. The only place I want this woman running is into my arms. But I'm not sure how to make that happen. She's a fucking queen. At twenty-five, she owns her own company. She's traveled the world. Worked with some of the most popular brands in existence.

She doesn't need me to provide for her or protect her. She's more than capable of doing those things on her own.

The only thing I have to offer her is myself. And we've already established that I'm an old, grumpy bastard compared to her. I've never been insecure or given a fuck what anyone thought. But with a goddess sprawled out beneath me, heaven in her eyes, I realize just how much better than me she is. She's the softest silk. I'm battered steel, left in the forge too long.

If I can't make her fall for me tonight, she'll fly out of my life tomorrow, taking the sun with her. So I'm playing with the only hand I've got. Sex. Submission. *Bliss*. I'll love her until she can't imagine not having me inside her. Until she's addicted to me, unable to make it through a single day without needing me inside her again. I'll possess her, consume her...ruin her. Whatever it takes to make her mine.

By the time morning comes, she'll belong to me, body and soul.

CHAPTER FIVE
TRINITY

"**Y**ou're mine, baby girl," Sage growls, a promise in his eyes that reflects in his gravelly voice. One big hand goes to the back of my head, his fingers plunging into my hair to tilt my head back. He wraps the other around my hip, moving me until I'm exactly where he wants me.

His mouth lands on mine a second later, his kiss hard and hungry.

I try to wrap my arms around his neck, but he pins my hands to the bed over my head. My stomach clenches as desire rushes through me in a flood. God, he's so damn confident and sexy. So sure of himself and what he's doing. I feel like I'm fumbling in the dark, stumbling through this. But somehow, he makes me feel sexy anyway, makes me feel like I'm perfectly safe here with him.

"Christ, sweet girl," he growls, kissing down my throat. His beard abrades my sensitive skin. "Knowing you want me to be your first makes me feel like a god."

With his body over mine, I think maybe he *is* a god.

His lips settle between my breasts, directly over my heart. He rests there for a minute, almost as if he's feeling the way my heart races for him. And then he turns his head slightly, pulling my nipple into the hot cavern of his mouth. He sucks hard.

A bolt of pleasure has my back bowing off the bed. I cry out his name, stunned at how incredible it feels. I never imagined that could feel so good or that I'd like it so much, but it does, and I do. I don't just feel it in my chest, but deep in my belly and clit, almost as if they're connected.

"I love the way you cry my name when I do that," he groans, releasing my nipple before claiming the other one. He bites down, dragging it through his teeth. The sharp sting blasts through me, making my stomach clench.

"Please, please," I sob, not quite sure what I'm begging for. More? Less? I ache everywhere. Every move he makes somehow makes it better and worse at the same time.

He kisses his way down my body, dragging my swimsuit down as he goes. I always thought I'd be nervous or feel shy the first time I was naked in front of a man. Even though I've been half naked in front of them for years, I thought being completely bare would make me nervous. But I'm not. It's different in a good way.

His sharp intake of breath lets me know he loves my body. So does the way he curses beneath his breath. His tongue dips into my belly button before sliding down my lower stomach. He places sweet kisses against my lower belly. It goes concave beneath his tongue, reacting to his touch just like the rest of me.

I'm on fire with need. There's so much of it I think I might explode apart.

"So sweet," he says. His hands go to my waist, his eyes meeting mine as he tugs my suit down over my hips. I lift my bottom, allowing him to tug the suit down to my thighs. His gaze settles on my center, his pupils flaring. "I bet you taste even better here. Like peaches and sticky sweet cream."

I startle when he buries his face in my center, inhaling deeply. His tongue peeks out a moment later, tasting me. I cry out, jerking beneath him. I want to spread my legs wider so he can do it again, but I'm trapped beneath him.

"Goddamn." He presses his lips to my mound, groaning. "I want to live between your legs, baby girl."

"Sage," I whisper, grasping onto the comforter like that's going to keep me from exploding into tiny pieces.

"I'm going to make you come on my tongue." He pulls back far enough to meet my gaze. His green eyes are dark, his expression ravenous. He tugs my suit down a little bit further, leaving it tangled around my thighs. I'm completely at his mercy, unable to move my legs more than a few inches. That probably shouldn't turn me on, but it sends desire ratcheting up until I feel like I might burst into flames if I don't get relief soon.

I whimper, wordlessly begging him to ease the burn.

"Don't be afraid," he murmurs, running a soothing hand down my thigh. Powerful emotion flares to life in his eyes, painting his handsome face with stark sincerity. "I won't hurt you, Trinity."

"I'm not afraid," I whisper back. Never once have I felt anything but desire for this man. People say he's an asshole, but they're wrong about him. He's blunt and honest, demanding. But there isn't a mean bone in his body. "I like it."

"Yeah?"

I nod my head, unable and unwilling to lie to him. "I like the way you feel on top of me," I say, holding his gaze. "I like knowing that you're in control." Every day of my life, it's up to me to make the hard decisions. Running a business is exhausting. There is so much responsibility settled squarely on my shoulders. Not today. For the first time in a long time, I get to just...be. "You make me feel so damn good, Sage. I love it."

A rumbling growl vibrates in his chest. His expression turns feral. He dips his head to place a soft kiss on my sex. And then he turns wicked. He spears his tongue through my folds, striking against my clit like a snake.

Intense pleasure shoots through me. A keening cry falls from my lips.

The sound he makes then is unholy hellfire. It's a warning and a promise all tangled up together. He shoves his hands beneath my bottom, lifting me toward his mouth. His tongue dances through my folds as if he's done this to me a thousand times before and knows exactly where I'm most sensitive. He hits every spot on the way to my clit.

I'm so wet it should probably be embarrassing, but it isn't. All I feel is bliss racing through my veins in powerful waves. They leave me stunned and gasping beneath him. I want to ask him if it's always like this, always this intense, but I can't form the words. They're stuck on my tongue, jumbled up in a thick ball. The only thing that emerges from between my lips is a stuttered sob.

"I wanted to take my time with you, but you taste so fucking good," he mumbles, releasing my hips to tear my suit the rest of the way down my legs. As soon as it's gone, he shoulders his way between my legs, forcing them wide to fit his big body between them. "I need more."

He doesn't give me time to brace myself or prepare to be eaten alive before he falls on me. His hands curl into tight fists on the bed as if he's afraid to touch me as he eats me. He's a wild animal, and I'm his prey, helpless to do anything but take the pleasure. He licks and sucks and bites, and all I can think is that he was right. That beard *does* feel better against the sensitive skin of my thighs. It feels like heaven.

"Sage!" I scream as pleasure builds to a fierce storm. It's so strong, I think it's going to rip me apart. I sob, trying to squirm away from him, but he won't let me go.

"Nu-uh, baby girl," he growls against my sex, his tongue circling my clit. "You tried to break me, now it's my turn. You stay right here until I'm done with you." He pulls my clit into his mouth, seaming his lips around it. One hand slips from beneath my ass, holding my lower lips open for him. His pointer finger circles my entrance before he presses it inside my opening. It's so thick, so good. He curls it up, striking against a spot inside I didn't even know existed.

Just like that, my body becomes his to command. I splinter apart, a scream of relief, of submission, breaking from my lips. Every muscle in my body locks up tight as wave after wave of euphoria crashes down on me like rapid-fire. I hear myself sobbing, but I can't seem to stop myself. I can't control the way my body shakes either. My entire world is a blur of swirling color, like I've tumbled through a kaleidoscope on my way into heaven.

The powerful feeling goes on forever before I fall limp.

Even then, my body trembles as aftershocks quake through me.

"That's it, sweet girl," Sage croons, his voice a deep rumble of sound as he runs his hands all over me, easing me back down to earth. "You look so beautiful when you're coming for me. God. I need inside you before I lose my mind."

The bed dips as he climbs to his feet. I whimper and reach out for him, wanting him back. He belongs between my legs. He fits there perfectly. I can't seem to make my body work to call him back to me though. It's all fuzzy, like it was after I had my wisdom teeth removed as a teenager. I hear him moving around and then the bed dips again.

A moment later, I'm back in his strong arms as they close around me. He shifts me up the bed, placing my head on a pillow. I finally manage to drag my eyes open to see him looming over me. The muscles in his arms and shoulders are taut as he holds himself up above me.

I rake my gaze down his body, shivering at the sight of him. He's completely naked and so damn beautiful. His body is so thick and powerful. I've seen naked men before. It's impossible not to see them in my line of work. But I've never seen anything like him before.

He really is like the redwood giants in California. Tall. Powerful. Rooted to the earth yet reaching into heaven. There's nothing little about him, nothing soft. He's all man, acres of golden, battered skin over roughly hewn muscles. Dark tattoos tell fragments of his story. I want to trace every single one, learn the secrets they hide.

"You keep looking at me like that, you won't be able to walk tomorrow, Trinity," he growls. He wraps a fist around his erection, working it up and down as he stares at me. A bead of precum wells from the tip, sliding down the broad head.

"You're not going to fit," I mumble, suddenly nervous as hell. His erection is as big as the rest of him. Even with his fist wrapped around it, there's room left. He's as big around as an aluminum can, and long enough to make me squirm. He's going to break me in half.

"Oh, I'll fit," he promises. His voice sounds like sandpaper, all gritty and rough. "Like I was born to ride you."

I'm not sure if he's just saying that to ease my mind or if he really means it, but I take a deep breath and nod, letting him know I trust him. Maybe I shouldn't. Maybe it's crazy to feel this sort of connection to someone I just met. But I *do* trust him. It's instinctive, natural, as if something inside me recognizes something inside of him. As if this part of me was meant to be his. I think I've been waiting my whole life to find him.

Our eyes meet as he settles over me, dragging my leg up over his hip. Emotion swirls through his gorgeous eyes, searing me to my soul. Whatever this is between us, he feels it too. I see the truth blazing in his eyes. He settles over me like a warm, familiar blanket. I'm completely surrounded by him, engulfed in his aura and the soft wash of emotion coursing through me with every powerful beat of my heart. Each one speaks directly to him, telling him what I can't put into words. It's peace and love and a sense of rightness I've never felt before.

"Sage," I whisper in awe, reaching up to touch his face with trembling hands.

"Trinity," he whispers back, turning his face to place a kiss to my palm. "My sweet little lamb."

"Make love to me," I plead.

"Are you sure?" he asks, swallowing hard. As if, now that the moment has come, *he's* nervous. But I'm not. Seeing that look in his eyes, feeling him on top of me...I've never been more certain of anything than I am of this. Of him.

Instead of answering, I slide my other leg up his thick thigh and hitch it around his hip, opening myself for him. I'm his for the taking. From the moment I saw him standing on the roof, I was his. My hands slide up his back, twining around his neck. I anchor myself to his big body, letting him root me to earth so I don't float away.

"Make me yours," I breathe.

"You're already mine," he growls, his expression turning fierce, possessive.

A soft moan climbs up my throat when he slides the head of his cock through my folds and then presses it to my opening. My heart thuds in my chest, anticipation pinging through me. My breathing picks up, my chest rising and falling rapidly. I'm not nervous though. Not anymore. I want this. I *need* this.

"Eyes on me, baby girl," he commands and then waits until I obey before he tilts his hips, sliding inside me.

Even though I didn't think it was possible, my opening stretches around his length, allowing him inside. A bite of pain brings tears to my eyes. It's sharp, like something tearing as he thrusts into me. As soon as he sees the tears in my eyes, his entire body goes still.

"I'm okay," I whimper.

"You're not." He groans like a miserable, wounded bear. "Fuck, I hate hurting you."

"Kiss me," I plead, desperately needing him to ground me again as a welter of emotions threaten to overwhelm me. There's pleasure and pain and something else, a vast shadow standing at the edge of everything, threatening to eclipse the entire world.

Love.

God, I think I'm falling in love with him.

He leans forward instantly, claiming my mouth in a searing kiss. Within seconds, the pain dulls and fades, leaving nothing but him and pleasure. As if he senses the change, he rocks his hips, his cock pushing in deeper. His tongue slips into my mouth, twining around mine in a sinuous, sensual dance I know instinctively. He kisses me deeply, his breath sweet as he breathes it into my lungs, taking the last of the pain from me.

His hips come to rest against mine a moment later. Once he's fully seated inside me, he moans against my lips and then lingers there. I take a breath, but the pain is truly gone. All I feel is full.

Good lord. He's so deep and I'm so damn *full.*

It feels incredible, like for the first time in my life, I'm finally whole.

I dig my nails into his shoulders, trying to pull him closer. I want to fuse our bodies together, imprint him in my skin so I never forget how perfect this moment feels. How incredible he is. If tonight is all I have of him, I want to remember it forever.

"God, Trinity," he breaths, breaking away from my lips. His eyes bore into me as he continues to hold himself still, letting me get used to the feel of him inside me. "Are you okay?"

"Perfect," I promise.

He scrutinizes my expression, checking to make sure I'm being truthful with him. Whatever he finds there seems to reassure him. The tightness around his eyes eases. He starts to move, sliding himself out before slowly pushing back inside.

I gasp his name, stunned at how good it feels.

"I know," he murmurs. "I feel it too, sweet girl." He circles his hips, grinding his pelvis against my clit before he pulls out in a slow glide. His head kicks back when he pumps back inside me, groaning my name. "I've never wanted anything the way I want you." He drags my leg higher up his hip. "Goddamn, I can't get enough of you."

He picks up speed, pumping in and out of me faster. I claw down his back, crying out in bliss. Every time he's all the way inside, he circles his hips, grinding against my clit in a way that makes my entire body react. Sweat breaks out on my skin, my head falling back against the pillows as I writhe beneath him.

"You feel that, Trinity?" he growls, raining kisses across my face and throat. "You feel how fucking perfect this little cunt feels wrapped around my cock?"

"Yes," I gasp. God, yes, I feel it. He fits inside me exactly right. It's unlike anything I've ever felt. Until now, I never understood why sex was such a big deal to people. It didn't make sense why people were so willing to go to such lengths to sleep with someone else. Until now, I never felt that sort of connection, that level of desperation. I feel it with him.

I'd fight for this. For him. Through hell, I think.

He's rough and gentle at the same time. Filthy praise and powerful groans leave his lips in an endless flood as he fucks me deeper, harder, until I'm wrecked beneath him and sobbing his name. Even then, he doesn't stop. He picks me up in his arms and settles back on his calves. I wrap around him like a blanket, clinging to his hard body, marveling all over again at how damn beautiful he is to me.

He guides me up and down his length, one hand tangled up in my hair, forcing me to watch him. I think he likes having my eyes on him, likes me to watch what he's doing to me. He lavishes attention on my breasts, moving from one to the other and then back again. Every time I feel his teeth in my skin, I cry out his name, pleasure bubbling higher and then higher again, until I feel like a pot on the verge of boiling over.

"I need you to come, baby girl," he groans.

"Please," I plead, afraid he's going to stop. I dig my fingers into his shoulders, using his body for leverage to push myself up and then slide back down. Digging my heels into his ass and my fingers into his shoulders. I push away from him and then slide back down, chasing the powerful jolts of pleasure shooting through me. Every time, his length grinds against that spot inside that leaves my head lolling on my shoulders. Pure ecstasy spirals higher, leaving me dazed and breathless.

"That's it," he growls when I rock against him again, greedy for more. "Take what you need from me, Trinity. Use me to get yourself there. I'm so hard for you it hurts. Fuck, it hurts."

His hands prowl across my ass, kneading my cheeks and spreading them apart as I move on him. His finger circles the tight ring of muscle, and I cry out. It feels so good. Way better than it should.

"This little hole is going to be mine too," he says, grinding his thumb against it. "Before morning, you'll be dripping my come from both holes, Trinity. Begging me to give you more."

"Oh god," I moan, certain I shouldn't want that nearly as much as I do. Too turned on to care what that says about me. I want this man however I can have him, in whatever way he wants to take me. I need it.

Leaving tomorrow is going to break me, I already know it.

I can't think about that though. It's impossible when he's inside me, fucking the breath from my lungs. The tangle of bliss rippling out from deep in my womb shrinks in on itself, sensation coiling tighter and tighter until each roll of my hips against his sends pleasure striking through me like a gong.

I'm helpless to do anything except chase the thrill, using his body to get myself off.

"You look good fucking yourself with my cock. Don't stop," he pants, bucking his hips against mine each time I drop down on him. It forces him deeper every time, until I feel him everywhere. "Take it, Trinity. Fuck. Take it all from me."

He slips his free hand between us, rolling his thumb across my clit.

I scream his name, coming apart at the seams. My hips buck wildly against him, pleasure raining down on me from every direction. It feels so good. God, I never want it to stop.

"Don't stop, don't stop," I chant over and over, unable to halt the flow of words as I writhe and shake my way through it, incapable of stopping.

His hands notch around my waist as he takes over, bouncing me up and down on him at a punishing pace. He snarls and curses, using me this time. He fucks me hard, pounding into me until I'm unraveling for him all over again.

"Oh, god, Sage," I gasp, my head falling back on my shoulders. "You're so deep. I feel you everywhere. Please, don't ever stop."

The last shred of his control snaps as I babble and plead. He moves like a raging storm, pumping into me so furiously the bed shakes beneath us, banging against the wall. I don't care if the whole hotel hears it and knows what's happening in here.

I scream again, another orgasm ripping through me before the second has even abated.

"Fuck!" he roars when my muscles clamp tight around him. He drops me down on him a final time and holds me there as his erection jerks inside me, his body going taut like a bowstring. He roars loudly as he comes, sending another wave of bliss through me. It blankets me in warmth, stealing away everything but him.

Somehow, I peel my eyes open, not wanting to miss a single second of this. The look of savage pleasure on his face is breathtaking. His head is kicked back, the tendons in his neck visible. His cheeks are flushed, and his eyes dilated as he bucks his hips without rhythm. He's like a god below me, fierce and mighty. Possession and devotion blaze in his eyes as his seed fills me with warmth.

Then and only then does it register that he's not wearing a condom. But somehow, I can't bring myself to feel regret. I've been on birth control for years to regulate my periods, and I want him just like this, raw, exposed. Beautiful.

So damn beautiful.

"Trinity," he whispers a moment later, his voice full of awe, of reverence. It reflects in his eyes too.

And I know that I don't want this to end when the sun rises. I want to be his, not just tonight but always. Whatever this is between us isn't supposed to end. It isn't temporary, fleeting. The way I feel about him is permanent, immutable. Like it was always supposed to be.

Like *we* were meant to be.

CHAPTER SIX
SAGE

"**C**ome on, sweet girl," I murmur, boosting Trinity up into my arms to carry her into the bathroom. I've already run water for her. I'm worried I was too rough with her at the end. Feeling her coming all over me and hearing her begging me not to stop sent me spiraling out of this dimension. *Nothing* has ever felt as good as being inside her does.

She's a limp, sweaty mess, her heart pounding against my chest as I cradle her carefully in my arms. As soon as she nestles in my arms with her face pressed against my throat, I fall in love with holding her like this. There's something that just feels right about taking care of her, as if she were intended to be mine to care for like this.

"I'm so sleepy," she murmurs as I carry her toward the bathroom. Like the rest of this room, it's opulent, extravagant to the extreme, with a massive tub and a waterfall shower. I wanted her to have the best for this photo shoot. Vanna intended for the shoot to happen in Central Park, but I wanted Trinity on the roof here, with NYC and the East River spread out below her. I'm not going to lie. Seeing her naked in this bathtub may have entered my mind a time or five when I booked the room for the indoor portion of the shoot, but I didn't have any expectations.

"I know you are." I run my lips across her sweaty forehead, lingering against her temple. I've never felt closer to anyone that I do to her. She's been in my life for a matter of hours, but she's already necessary for my survival. Making love to her was, hands down, the best experience of my life. Knowing I'm the one who pleased her makes me feel like a god.

I already know nothing and no one will ever touch me like she did. She's my one, the reason for my existence. I was born to make love to her. The tight grip of her cunt around my cock, the way her body molds to mine...it's insane how perfectly she fits against me, like two disparate puzzle pieces locking together to form one whole unit.

"Easy, sweet girl," I croon, lowering her carefully into the tub.

She moans as the hot water and soapy bubbles submerge her all the way to her neck. I hold her carefully so she doesn't slip beneath the water as I climb into the massive garden tub behind her, sliding her backward into my arms.

"Mmm," she moans, settling against me with a sweet sigh that hits me right in the heart.

For several long moments, neither of us speaks. I just hold her, listening to the sweet sounds that escape her lips. She's mewling like a happy little kitten. If my heart didn't already belong to her, hearing those adorable purring sounds would have done it. But my heart is already hers. I think it's been hers since I saw her staring back at me from my computer screen.

"I was too rough with you," I murmur when she shifts in my arms and immediately grimaces. Regret fills me, pulsing like a second heartbeat in my chest. Fuck. I took her too hard, hurt her.

"No," she says, turning her head until her glassy eyes meet mine. "You were perfect."

"You're sore."

"Just a little," she promises, snuggling up to me again with her head on my shoulder. She drapes her hand across my opposite shoulder, humming. "But I think everyone is a little sore their first time, aren't they?"

"Wouldn't know," I say. "Yours is the only cherry I've ever popped."

"Really?"

"Mmhmm. I told you this isn't something I do, lamb. I haven't thought about a woman in years, and I don't want to think about one while you're in my arms either." I don't want to think about anyone else, period. What I've done before doesn't even compare. And whoever she was doesn't even matter because I'll never be with anyone else again. It'll be Trinity for me or no one.

"Sorry." She stirs on my lap, fidgeting. She doesn't drop it though. "You're so handsome. You could have anyone. I guess I'm just surprised."

"Don't want anyone else," I growl. "You think I'm a manwhore?"

"No, of course not," she rushes to say. "I'm just..." She huffs out an adorable breath. "I don't know what I'm thinking. You made me feel so good. I guess I just assumed you had a lot of practice."

"Ah," I say, understanding. "No. I've been married to my job for most of my life. I've lived like a nomad since I finished college. It didn't leave a lot of time for dating, and no one ever interested me enough before now to make me want to change that. But I know how to make you feel good, baby girl. Your body tells me exactly what I need to know."

"It does?"

I smile at her tone. She's so fucking innocent.

"Mmhmm." I run my hand down her arm in demonstration, trailing my fingers across the side of her breast. She shivers almost immediately, melting against me. "See? When you like something, your whole body lights up. When you don't, you tense."

"Oh." She falls quiet again. The silence is comfortable though, easy. She isn't someone who needs to fill every moment with noise to escape her thoughts. Instead, she settles into them, completely at ease with herself and the moment. Silence isn't foreign to her. It's a familiar, appreciated friend.

I'm the same way. There's beauty in solitude and comfort in silence. I have no demons haunting me, no regrets plaguing me. My whole life, I've gone where I wanted, did what I wanted. I may have been rigid and unyielding, but I wasn't a bastard, blowing through life like a hurricane. I focused on my job, my art, and that was always enough for me. I didn't need the thrill of the chase, of drugs, or alcohol, or any of that shit. So long as I had my camera, I was content.

But I find myself eager to fill the silence now, to know every thought Trinity has, no matter how fleeting or small. I want to know her in every way it's possible to know someone else, and I want her to know me the same way. We won't have secrets from one another. Whatever she wants to know, I'll tell her. Happily.

"I can't believe Georgia never mentioned that you were her uncle," she says a few moments later.

"That's Georgia." I smile. "When she decided to model, I offered to help her. She told me I wasn't allowed to tell anyone that we were related."

Trinity laughs quietly, her body shifting against mine. "I won't tell her you broke her rule if you don't."

"She really likes you."

"Yeah?" I hear the smile in her voice, the affection. "I like her too. She's a lot of fun to be around, and she's absolutely gorgeous. She told you about me?"

"She talked about you."

"Oh. It's kind of funny," she says, running her finger through a pile of bubbles.

"What is?"

"That she doesn't want anyone to know her uncle is the photographer virtually every model aspires to work with. It wasn't like that for me. My brother plays hockey."

"He does a little bit more than that. His team has won the Cup four times in the last eight years." Most teams are fortunate to win once in a decade. Winning four in eight years is a helluva feat, especially for a team that's considered new by most anyone's standards.

"You're a fan?"

"Of hockey? Yes. Of the Predators? Afraid not, lamb. I'm a Chicago fan," I say.

"Booooo."

I chuckle at her loyalty. "I gotta support the home team."

"You're from Chicago?"

"Born and raised."

"Huh," she says like she's surprised. "I guess I just assumed that your family lived here in New York since that's where Georgia grew up."

"Marnie attended school at Juilliard and never left," I explain. "Ty followed behind her not long later. I spend more time here than anywhere else, but Chicago has always been home to me."

"That's how I feel about Nashville. I've been in Los Angeles for a while, but the south is just in my blood," she says and then laughs quietly. "But that's not where I was going with this conversation. I was trying to say that it's funny to me that Georgia wanted to do this completely on her own. I was the exact opposite. When I first decided to pursue modeling, it was because I was tired of seeing size zero models. I was at a photo shoot with Gray one day, and of course the models posing with him were all tiny, which is not his type. When I mentioned it, the photographer laughed at the thought of posing this hockey star with a bigger woman."

"Prick," I mutter, running my hand up and down her back again. Fuck men who think big women aren't beautiful. In my experience, they're usually assholes unworthy of any woman, let alone a goddess like the one in my arms.

"That's what Gray said!"

I'm liking her brother more and more by the minute.

"Anyway, it frustrated me, so I decided I wanted to do something about it. Gray helped pave the way for me. He'd just won their first Stanley Cup. No one wanted to tell him no. Without having him backing me, I probably never would have made it as far as I did."

"You're wrong," I say softly. "He may have gotten your foot in the door, but *you* showed the world that you belonged right where you were. You did the hard part, lamb. He just supported you because he loves you."

"You think so?" She twists to look at me over her shoulder.

"I know so." I brush wet tendrils of hair away from her face. "You're beautiful, talented, smart, and sexy as hell. You're also passionate about representation and dedicated to carving out a place for plus-size women in a business where they've never been welcomed. You didn't get here by riding on his coattails, Trinity. You worked your ass off to earn your success. And you *have* earned it."

She blinks wide eyes at me, her expression soft. "That means a lot coming from you."

"I capture what you give me. That's all."

"Okay, Mr. Modesty," she says, sassing me. "How many awards have you won?"

"I don't do it for the awards. Truthfully, I don't even show up at half of them," I admit. "Having people kiss my ass never interested me."

"Why do you do it?"

"Anyone with a camera can take a photo, but it takes work to create a piece of art using a live subject. I like the challenge," I say. "And the traveling doesn't suck either."

"What's your favorite place?" she asks, moaning when I dig my fingers into the muscles in her upper back.

"Right here."

"New York City is pretty amazing."

"I'm not talking about New York, lamb," I murmur, brushing her hair away from her shoulders. I trail my lips up and down the side of her neck before wrapping my tongue around the shell of her ear. "I'm talking about right here, right now. In this bath-tub with you."

"Oh," she whispers, though it comes out like a moan. "I kind of like it too."

"Yeah?"

I slide my hand down her belly, groaning at the way she responds to my touch. Her stomach quivers beneath my palm, her body melting against mine. She whimpers, practically writhing in my lap. Her legs inch open in invitation.

I take it, slipping my hand between her thighs. She's wet and swollen, her clit begging for attention. Jesus. She's so fucking wet.

"Yeah. God, Sage. That feels so damn good."

"Good," I growl, nipping at her ear. "I want you addicted to me, Trinity. This body belongs to me. No one else touches you."

"Yes!" She tilts her hips into my hand, her legs splayed wide for me. "Yes, it's yours."

"Damn right it is," I tell her. "I'm the one who gets you off when you need it, the one you call when you ache. I'll keep you satisfied, baby girl. Every fucking day until you can't imagine not having me in you."

I play with her until she's crying out my name and coming all over me, fascinated by how freely she gives herself to me. She doesn't shy away or try to hide a single second of her pleasure. She submerges herself in it, diving in with both feet like I'm coming to learn she does with everything. She does nothing halfway. When she's in, she's all in.

That passion, that spark...*goddamn*. It calls to me like Siren song, luring me in deeper. Deeper. Until I'm absolutely certain she's what's been missing from my life for so long. I feel more alive with her in my arms than I ever have before. And I don't even have to ask to know she feels more alive in mine. I watched her blaze to life like a supernova exploding.

Her nails make crescent-shaped marks in my forearms as she falls into a powerful orgasm, crying out my name. I work her through it, kissing all over her neck and shoulders, telling her how fucking perfect she is. I'm completely bewitched by her, and I don't want it to ever end.

As soon as she catches her breath, she turns in my arms, straddling my lap. Her hands delve into my hair, her lips seeking mine. A frustrated sob bubbles from her lips as she tries to get me inside her only for me to halt her. It's like a switch flipped inside her, one I'm not sure I understand. She's frantic with need, desperate to feel me inside her again.

"Please, Sage," she cries, grinding against me. "Please."

"Baby girl, lamb," I gasp, trying like hell to slow her down before she hurts herself. "You need a break."

"No, I need you!"

"Fuck," I growl, and then swat her on the ass when she tries to get me inside her again.

She cries out my name, pulling at my hair.

I manage to subdue her long enough to stand with her in my arms. She's shaking with need, sobbing my name. Water sloughs off us in a flood, soaking the floor around the bathtub, but I don't fucking care. I step carefully over the edge, waiting until I'm sure I'm not going to slip and fall with her in my arms, and then I storm toward the bedroom.

She lands on the bed on her stomach, that round ass in the air. I smack it, watching the way it bounces and jiggles beneath my palm. My dick is standing straight up, straining toward her. Eager. So fucking eager.

And even though I had good intentions, she wrecks them with her ass in the air and my name on her lips. Just completely annihilates them. I'm so far under her spell, I can't deny her. It physically hurts to try.

"Sage, Sage," she chants.

I come down over her, covering her body with mine. My teeth sink into the curve where her neck meets her shoulder. She sobs my name again, writhing on the bed beneath me. I press my knee between her legs, wrenching them open.

She screams when I thrust into her, hard. Harder than I intended.

"Shit." I still inside her, kissing her where I just bit. "Sorry, lamb."

"No," she whispers. "More, please. More."

Fucking hell. She's a seductress, a temptress, writhing beneath me, begging for me to give her what she wants. Whatever has her so worked up, I feel it too. Like a weight pressing down on me, demanding I give in to it, give her what she needs. My body is hers to command.

I fuck her hard, one fist wrapped in her hair, the other playing between her legs. She's a dream beneath me, liquid sex. So hot and wet, so fucking horny for it. For me.

My balls smack against her ass with every deep thrust, stinging. She cries out my name every time, louder and louder, until she's wailing it into the room.

We fall together in a mess of cum and sticky bubbles. The sheets are damp beneath us, twisted all up in the bed. She's completely wrecked, but she clings to me like her life depends on it. As if she's afraid I'll slip away like smoke.

"I'm right here," I murmur, pulling her into my arms. "I'm not going anywhere."

The thing is...I didn't count on her being the one to disappear.

Chapter Seven
TRINITY

I'm a coward. I know I am before I ever slip out of Sage's room at sunrise. But I slip out anyway. Because I know if I have to say goodbye to him, I'll fall apart. I'll beg him for more. He was honest with me about what this was. He wanted one night. I can't be greedy and ask for more now that the end has arrived. It wouldn't be fair to him.

A million times over the course of the day and night, I wanted to ask. Every time he said I belonged to him, I wanted to beg him to mean it permanently. Every time he held me in his arms, I wanted to tell him how I feel about him. But I didn't. I was so damn afraid he'd tell me no and what little time I had with him would dwindle to nothing. It would disappear in a puff of smoke, and I'd be left with a broken heart.

One night isn't enough for me. In the space of a day, he's come to occupy every empty space in my heart, filling it full of himself. I've fallen head over heels in love with him and how sweet he is to me.

With how quiet he can be, and how growly. With the way he looks at me like he's never seen anything more beautiful. With the way he talks to me about my dreams for my business, as if he truly understands how important it is to me. With the way he makes love to me. Even when he's pounding into me so hard he knocks me breathless, he's protective and caring.

He was so worried he'd hurt me the first time. And the second time. By the third time, he knew better. The fourth time...*God*, the fourth time. I never knew anal sex could be beautiful. I always thought it would be dirty and uncomfortable and awkward. With him, it was nothing like that. He made it so damn amazing.

God, lamb. You have no idea how beautiful you look with your ass in the air for me. I want to photograph you like this, just so I can wake up to this image every day.

Do you like it, lamb? Do you feel how tight this little hole is gripping me? You don't want me to leave it, do you?

That's it, lamb. Goddamn, I wish you could see what I see right now. You're so fucking perfect.

Ah, God, baby girl. You keep letting me take you like this, I won't ever let you leave this bed.

Every muscle in my body aches, but I don't regret a second of it. If losing the ache means forgetting even a second of our night together, I'll keep the ache forever. It'll be like having a little piece of him with me, one no one else will ever have.

He's everything I've ever wanted and so many things I never thought to ask for in a man. I don't think there is another one like him out there. He isn't just a great photographer. He's an incredible man. The only one I've ever wanted. The only one I can imagine spending the rest of my life loving.

But I'm terrified if I tell him how I feel, our one magical night will end badly. Instead of perfect memories of a beautiful man, I'll spend the rest of my life remembering him breaking my heart into tiny pieces. I'm not ready to face that pain.

So I don't ask him for more. And I don't say good-bye.

I slip back down to my room, the hallway a watery blur the whole way. I was supposed to meet Vanna this morning for final approval of the photos before I fly back home, but I send her a text, telling her something has come up and I have to leave immediately. Whatever photos they choose will be amazing, I'm sure of it. How can they not be when Sage is the one who took them?

Naturally, she texts back immediately. I don't think she ever sleeps. She's worried about me, wants to make sure everything is okay. I feel horrible for lying to her, but I can't tell her the truth. *I fell in love with the photographer and now I'm too afraid to face him* doesn't roll off the tongue.

Besides, sleeping with Sage wasn't particularly professional. I don't want it to reflect badly on her, Le CRV, or any of the other winners. They deserve nothing but admiration for everything they do.

Once I reassure her that everything is fine, I take the fastest shower I've ever taken and then throw all of my things into my bag. I still have hours before I have to be at the airport, but I check out of the hotel and catch a cab anyway. The city is just starting to wake up as we creep toward La Guardia in Queens. It all passes by in a blur for me.

Eventually, the cabbie gives up trying to make polite conversation and we make the drive in total silence. After a chaotic day, silence has always been a welcome companion. Today, it seems loud, abrasive. I want Sage's gruff, rumbling voice back. I want the sound of his heart beating beneath my ear. I want to hear him muttering gibberish in his sleep. I want him.

For the first time ever, I dread going back to work. Everyone will want to know how it went or what I did. They'll have a million questions about what it's like to work with Sage. I won't be able to hide it once the photos come out. Le CRV will hype his involvement because nothing sends magazines flying of the shelf faster than attaching his name to a project.

God, what am I supposed to say to Georgia?

I spent an amazing night with your uncle and fell in love with him, but please don't ever mention his name because I might crumble if you do?

She'll just love hearing that.

"We're here, lady," the cabbie says, claiming my attention.

I look up through bleary eyes, blinking when I realize we're outside of the airport, blocking other cars from pulling into the loading zone. A police officer is scowling at the cab as if he's telling us to hurry it up before he boots us out of the line.

"Sorry." I quickly grab a handful of bills out of my purse to cover the fare and tip and then climb out with my bags. Since the trip was so short, I didn't bring much with me.

The officer loses interest as soon as my driver puts the car in drive.

By the time I make it through security, I'm even more stressed out and exhausted. The airport is a mess of activity like usual. Every seat at my gate is already taken by passengers on the flight leaving in an hour. I find a seat at the adjoining gate and plop down, staring out at the tarmac.

I don't know how long I stare out, caught in my own mind and memories of last night. But when my phone buzzes with an incoming notification, the sun is up and shining brightly. I fish my cell from my pocket, shaking my head when I see a message from my brother, Gray.

Gray: Are you alive? Do I need to send search and rescue? You haven't answered my last eighty-four texts.

He's so overdramatic. I had two missed texts from him this morning, and one from our mom. I didn't text either of them back. Mom is still sleeping, and I figured Gray would be at practice by now. He has a home game tonight.

Me: You texted me twice.

Gray. Oh, good. You are alive. I'll cancel the bloodhounds.

I'm still typing a response when he calls.

"Did the photoshoot run over or something?" he asks as soon as I answer.

"No. I just didn't have my phone," I say, which is technically true. It was in my room all day...and I was in Sage's. I leave that part out. Some things, my brother doesn't need to know. And I don't want to cry in the airport. I can do that when I get home.

"You always have your phone. It's like your security blanket."

"You were the one with a security blanket, not me," I remind him.

"Do me a favor? Don't tell my super-hot wife that. She's already way out of my league."

"Yeah, she is," I say, smiling for the first time all day. Somehow, he always manages to make me feel better. Probably because he's completely crazy. But we can't all be normal, or the world would be boring, so I love him anyway. He's the best brother.

"You're supposed to be on my side," he complains. "But I'll let this one slide since I'm on her side too. Are you at the airport?"

"Yeah, just waiting on my flight."

"You're there early. Your flight doesn't leave for another four hours."

"It got moved up," I lie.

"No, it didn't. I checked ten minutes ago."

Crap.

"Stalker."

"It's not stalking when you're my sister, Trin," he says, his voice firm. "What's going on? You sound weird and you're acting weird. Did the shoot not go well?"

"It went fine."

"You're a shit liar. What happened?"

"Nothing happened," I huff.

His silence is deafening.

"You are so annoying," I complain.

"Obviously. I'm your brother. It's in the job description. So cut the shit and stop trying to distract me. What happened?"

"I slept with Sage," I blurt, a little too loudly because everyone in the immediate vicinity goes quiet. Crap. I duck my head to hide my face like that's going to keep them from knowing I'm the one who said it.

"What the fuck?" Gray growls. I told him that Sage requested the shoot as soon as the party ended the other night, so he already knows exactly who I'm talking about. "Did he force himself on you? I'll pull his balls out through his throat and then hide his body under the ice. I knew he was suspicious. What's his last name again? Did you call the police? Fuck. Where's Kelsey when I actually do need to hide a body? I'm going to fucking murde—"

"I'm in love with him," I say, tears welling in my eyes at the thought of Gray and Sage fighting. Gray means well, but the last thing I want is for the brother I adore to kill the man I love. "He didn't do anything wrong. He's amazing, Gray. He was so good to me."

"If he's so amazing, why the fuck are you crying in the airport?" he growls, not mollified.

"Because I'm an idiot!" I cry.

"Well, I mean..." he says, which is the same thing I've been saying to him for years when he tells me he's an idiot for doing whatever he did to get himself in trouble—it happens surprisingly often. He's the dumbest smart person I know. Telling him that always makes him laugh. But when I don't laugh, he sighs. "You aren't an idiot, Trin. You're one of the smartest people I know."

"No, I'm not."

"Yes, you are."

"I snuck out of his room, packed all my stuff, and fled to the airport," I say, sniffling.

"Which we will be discussing later," someone growls from behind me. No, not someone. *Sage.*

Oh my gosh. Sage is here.

I gasp and jump to my feet, spinning around in shock. He's standing directly behind my seat, his arms crossed, scowling like a handsome devil. His hair is pulled back away from his face, his clothing—the same he wore yesterday—wrinkled. But it's him. He's really here right now.

I burst into tears.

"Sweet lamb," he says, his rumbling voice soft. His expression softens too, melting like he finds it impossible to be angry with me. "What am I going to do with you?"

"W-w-what are you d-doing h-here?"' I sob as he circles around the short row of airport seats to me. Everyone in the area is openly staring now but I don't even care.

"Who is that? Is Sage there? What's going on?" Gray demands.

I try to answer him, but only manage a string of incoherent gibberish.

Once Sage reaches my side, he plucks the phone from my hands. He holds my gaze as he brings it to his ear. "Gray, it's Sage. Sage Grimes, your future brother-in-law. She's going to have to call you back after she explains to me why she ran off."

My mouth is hanging wide open, but I can't seem to close it again. He just told my brother that he's going to marry me. Holy crap. If this is a dream, I never want to wake up.

Sage listens for a moment to whatever my brother says, his expression not changing. His seafoam green eyes never leave my face. "Yeah. Will do."

Gray is still talking when he disconnects.

"You need to call your brother back later," he says, shoving my phone into his pocket. He barely has it out of the way before he's pulling me into his arms. He holds me tight, my face pressed to the hollow of his throat, his strong arms surrounding me.

For several long moments, we stay just like that as I cry it out. I try to keep myself from hoping he's here because he loves me too, but little seeds take root and sprout anyway. He introduced himself to my brother as his future brother-in-law. I'm pretty sure that means he plans to be around for a while.

The longer he holds me, the bigger those seeds grow. Until the last few hours of turmoil seem like a bad dream. Eventually, I manage to get myself under control. I probably look like a hot mess, but there's nothing I can do about that now. Besides, he's seen more of me than anyone else ever has before...and loved every second of it. He left no doubts about that last night.

Please, baby Jesus. I'll never ask for anything again if you let me keep this man.

"I can't believe you're really here," I whisper.

"Of course I'm here. You're here." He studies me intently as he tucks strands of hair behind my ears and then dries my tears with his thumbs. Once he's done, he cups my cheeks in his palms. "You okay now, baby girl?"

"I..." I trail off before I can apologize. He thinks I do that too much, which is probably true. "What are you doing here, Sage?"

"I just told you. You're here. Where else would I be?"

"I...don't understand."

"I couldn't let you leave, lamb."

"Why not?"

He hesitates for a minute like he's searching for an answer. The instant inspiration strikes, I see it in his gaze. Triumph. Satisfaction. He tugs me closer to him, his expression dark and heated. "Because you agreed to let me take you out and show you off. I haven't gotten to do that yet, so our date isn't over."

The rough growl of his voice rolls over me like a hot wind, setting me on fire. Those seeds of hope spread throughout my entire body, obliterating every little bit of heartache and doubt. Until I feel like I'm floating six inches off the ground. His hands on my body are the only thing tethering me to this dimension.

"We definitely can't have that," I whisper, pressing up against him, not caring who sees or what they think. When he wraps his arms around me, the last few pieces of my heart stitch themselves back together.

"Definitely not," he growls against my lips.

It's a long time before he stops kissing me.

It's even longer before we talk.

CHAPTER EIGHT
SAGE

"You know I can't stay here forever," Trinity whispers, lifting her head to look at me. We're tangled up in the bed, exactly where we're supposed to be. When I woke up to find her gone this morning, I damn near had a panic attack. The kid at the front desk refused to tell me anything, but when Vanna texted to tell me Trinity was flying home and would miss our meeting, I was able to put the pieces together myself.

It took me exactly five seconds to decide I was going after her. I bought a ticket for the first available flight to Los Angeles, worried she may have switched to an earlier flight, and then jumped in a taxi. I didn't pack anything. Didn't even stop to put on underwear or socks. The thought of her disappearing from my life had my heart in my throat the entire way to the airport.

Part of me wanted to spank her ass for trying to slip away. The other part was seriously fucking worried that maybe she didn't feel the same way and I misunderstood. Every time we got close to touching on the subject of her leaving last night, she practically threw herself into my arms, demanding I make love to her again, as if she couldn't bear to discuss it.

I shouldn't have let her get away with it.

I should have told her that I'm in love with her.

Seeing her crying in the airport damn near brought me to my knees. I knew right then and there that she loves me too. I still don't know why she decided to sneak out without talking to me, but she feels the same way I do, I'd stake my life on it.

"I know," I murmur, running my hand down to her ass. "I kind of thought I might go to Los Angeles with you, lamb."

"Like, to visit?"

"I was thinking longer."

Her eyes grow big enough to fall out of her head, which makes me smile.

"Your life is in Los Angeles. I'm not going to ask you to sacrifice it for me," I murmur. "I'm not going to ask you to pick up your life and move for me, baby girl. Your business is too important to you. So I'll move in with you."

"You want to move in with me?" she whispers.

I smile again, shaking my head. She's a mess in the best way. "I have to move in with you," I say instead of telling her that.

"You do?" She narrows her eyes on me, suddenly suspicious. "Why?"

"Because I have this problem," I say, kneading her ass in my hands, remembering how fucking incredible it felt to take her here last night. We will be doing that again, just as soon as I manage to get her pregnant. She may not realize it yet, but she may already be carrying my kid. We didn't use protection. The thought of having a barrier between us doesn't appeal to me at all. Getting this woman pregnant would be the greatest blessing in my life right next to her.

"What problem?"

"The one where I slept with you in my arms last night and now I can't ever sleep without you in them again," I growl, running my nose up the soft plane of her cheek. "You ruined me, sweet lamb. I need you now. Forever."

"Sage," she whispers, her eyes welling with tears.

"I love you, Trinity," I say, rolling until she's on her back beneath me and I'm hovering over her. My hair falls forward, narrowing my world to just her. Exactly the way it should be. This woman is everything I never knew I wanted, and everything I'd die to protect. The only place she'll ever run again is to me, into *my* arms. Exactly where she belongs.

"Sage," she whispers again, crying openly now. "I love you too."

"Is that why you ran this morning, lamb? You thought I wouldn't feel the same?"

She nods. "You asked for one night," she says, her bottom lip quivering in a way that makes my chest ache. She's too beautiful for tears yet is somehow ravishing with them slipping down her cheeks. "I was so afraid you'd tell me you only wanted one night. I didn't want my last memory with you to be you breaking my heart."

"Never, baby girl," I vow, leaning down to capture her lips with mine. I kiss her gently, tasting her tears. "Your heart belongs to me now. I'll guard it with my life. No one will ever break it or make you cry without answering to me."

"You're making me cry right now!" she cries, making me chuckle.

I deepen the kiss, distracting her. Her arms slide around my shoulders, anchoring her body to mine. For long moments, we lose ourselves in one another, making up for the painful hours she wasn't right here where she belongs. That won't happen again. Wherever she goes, I follow. Even if it's to the ends of the earth.

Her leg curves around my hip, opening her up to me in silent invitation. She needs me again. I need her too. It's physically painful not to be inside her. Nothing has ever felt as right as it does when she's wrapped around me, pleading with me not to stop.

We both gasp on the first deep thrust, falling still. Reveling. Last night, there was a hint of urgency to our furious lovemaking, as if we were both trying to gorge ourselves on one another. As if we were both afraid our time was slowly running out. When we got back here from the airport, there was the urgency to be connected again. That's gone now. This time, I take her slow, making love to her until we're both dripping sweat, both lost in love and found in one another.

I tell her over and over that I love her. It's as if speaking those words out loud freed us both. We kiss and touch and fuck, until we're both trembling on the edge. I send her over with my hands tangled with hers, our lips locked together.

Her cry of completion dances across my lips and spills into my soul.

I spill into her, giving her all of me. My heart, my soul, my seed. Everything.

"You really want to move to Los Angeles?" she asks a long time later, her voice soft and sleepy. I'm guessing she didn't sleep much last night. She probably laid awake all night, stressing herself out about leaving this morning. I feel like an asshole for sleeping through it. She wore me out yesterday.

"I'd follow you to hell if that's what you asked of me, lamb," I murmur, pulling her over on top of me and then dragging the covers up over us. I'll be missing our meeting with Vanna. She'll understand.

I looked through the photos on the way to the airport this morning. They're incredible. Especially the ones of Trinity splayed across the white chaise like a wanton sacrifice. She's pure sex, so fucking beautiful there's not a chance in hell I'll ever let Vanna publish those photos. They're mine. Just for me.

But the last one I took of her on the roof, that one is pure gold. As soon as Vanna sees it, I know she'll agree. My girl looks stunning. Not a single part of it needs retouching.

"What about your job?" Trinity asks, snuggling up against my chest.

"I can take pictures anywhere," I murmur. "There is no shortage of models in Los Angeles. I can work from there as easily as I can from Chicago or New York."

"You love traveling."

"I do, but I've seen the world, lamb. I've been everywhere and done a little of everything. And in all that time, I never found the one thing I was looking for. I never found you."

"Sage," she whispers.

"It's true. We can travel on your schedule but traveling won't ever complete me the way holding you does. You're my soul, sweet lamb. I go where you go. The rest will sort itself out eventually," I say, meaning it. We may have to make adjustments, but we'll make them together. We'll figure out the future together. There is no rule that says we have to figure it out right now. We have a lifetime to get it right. And I plan to spend every spare moment of that lifetime with this woman in my arms.

Precisely where she belongs.

"I can't believe this is really happening," she whispers. "I can't believe you love me."

"How could I not?" I ask, tipping my head to place a kiss on her crown. "You're everything good in this world, lamb. *Everything*." And I'm not nearly crazy enough to let her go now that I've found her. Taking pictures is what I learned to do but loving her is what I was born to do. When I die, that's what I want the world to remember. This woman and the beauty she brought into my life. The purpose and the joy.

"I feel the same way about you, Sage."

"Yeah?"

"Yeah," she whispers as she drifts off in my arms, perfectly content.

I smile at how sweet she is. This woman... God, this woman is going to be the greatest adventure I've ever had. And I can't fucking *wait* to see where it takes us.

EPILOGUE
TRINITY

Five Years Later

"Little one," I murmur, running my hand across my belly. "Your foot is digging into mommy's ribcage."

"Sowwie, mommy," Sariah says from beside me, lifting her dark head from the pillow. We're in mine and Sage's bed, watching Aladdin for the thousandth time this month. Her eyes meet mine and she smiles, completely melting my heart. With her seafoam green eyes and charcoal hair, she looks so much like Sage, it's unreal. She has his smile too.

Sage is wrapped tightly around her little finger. He has been since the moment we found out I was pregnant with her four years ago. It took us a year to finally get pregnant. We saw a fertility specialist when it didn't happen right away. I thought Sage was going to jump across the desk and down his throat when he suggested that losing weight might help.

It took weeks to convince my husband that the doctor wasn't being critical of me. Sage is so protective, and he worships my body. The thought of anyone trying to change a single thing about me makes him a little crazy. To him, I'm perfect. And that's not just something he says. He means it.

Eventually, I managed to convince him to give the doctor another shot, but somewhere between that first appointment and the second, we finally got pregnant. And my grumpy photographer fell like a ton of bricks for the little girl growing in my belly. There has never been a more devoted daddy or husband than ours. Sariah and I live a fairy-tale life. He spoils us every single day in a million different ways.

People thought Sage and I were crazy to get married so quickly after meeting, but we haven't regretted a single moment. I don't know if it was fate or destiny or divine intervention, but we were meant to find one another. We were meant to complete one another.

We've traveled the world together and turned my agency into one of the premier modeling agencies in the state of California. We've laughed and loved and learned one another inside out. My life is brighter because he's in it. Even after five years together, he still finds ways to make me fall in love with him all over again. I don't think I'll ever stop.

"Ouch," I say, grimacing as another little toe digs into my ribcage.

"I didn't do nufin, mommy!" Sariah promises, throwing her hands up in the air as if to show it wasn't her.

"I know, lovebug." I massage my side, flinching. "One of your baby brothers has his tiny little toes between my ribs."

"Oh no," Sariah whispers. Her little face scrunches up in concern and then she places her hand on my stomach beside mine. "Baby brudder, you hab to stop huwting mommy."

Sage's soft chuckle rolls over me, pulling my gaze away from our daughter. I find him standing in the doorway, snapping photos of us. He lowers the camera, his gaze raking over me. That's all it takes to make my stomach flip and my heart pick up speed. Even though I'm almost eight months pregnant, he still looks at me like he's going to die if he isn't inside me right now.

"Don't move," he says, lifting the camera to take another photo.

"What are you doing?" I ask, smiling at him. "You're supposed to be working." He has a studio in the basement where he does all of the behind-the-scenes things like developing photos and editing them. After we had Sariah, he stopped taking a lot of jobs. Traveling without us just made him grumpy. I was worried he'd come to resent us, but if anything, I think the opposite is true. He loves all the extra time he gets with us, and we travel as a family whenever we can.

Well, we did until we found out I was pregnant again. Our twin boys, Samuel and Soren, are due in six weeks, though my doctor says we should expect them at any time. They're both measuring big for their gestational age...which means I'm huge.

Sage doesn't seem to mind. If anything, seeing me pregnant makes him want me even more. He loves seeing me grow as our babies grow. He makes love to me every morning and again most nights. The things he does to me... God, that first magical night doesn't even compare to how good it is now. He knows my body, inside and out. He's a wicked, wicked man.

I thought men were supposed to lose stamina as they aged, but mine hasn't. Some nights, he takes me over and over again. Until I'm pleading for mercy because my entire body is so sensitive every touch feels like another orgasm. I love every minute of it. And I know he does too. He's so vocal in the bedroom. I never have to ask to know what he's thinking or feeling. He tells me without reservation or shame.

"I am working," he says, lifting his camera to take another picture.

"On what?"

"A maternity shoot for my gorgeous wife," he murmurs, snapping another picture when Sariah lays her head on my belly to talk to her brothers. Surprisingly, they've stopped jabbing me in the ribs with their toes. One of them is busy kicking the side of Sariah's face now, making her giggle.

"Sage," I whisper. He's always taking pictures of me. Most, he refuses to share with anyone. He says those are just for him. I never thought I'd pose nude until him. But I've posed for him more than once. He keeps those photos under lock and key. I can always tell when he's been looking at them though. He gets so worked up he can't wait to get inside me again.

"Don't *Sage* me, baby girl. You look too beautiful not to photograph."

"I'm in a sports bra and bike shorts. I haven't even brushed my hair!"

"And you look more beautiful now than ever," he says, moving closer. He continues snapping photos of me and Sariah. She's so used to him taking pictures that she doesn't even bat a lash or pay him any attention most of the time. I think she may be more well photographed than the royal babies at this point.

"Sage," I whisper again, melting.

"When our babies are grown and you're missing them, you won't look back at the pictures and worry because you weren't dressed, lamb. You'll look back and smile at the memories," he murmurs. "You'll have a thousand other chances to take pictures looking like a goddess in your makeup and fancy clothes. But you only get to be the goddess pregnant with our boys for a little while longer. And I want you to be able to remember every moment of it."

"You're going to make me cry!"

He prowls toward me, not stopping until he's right beside the bed. He sets the camera on the nightstand and leans down over me. His long hair hangs like a curtain around his face, blocking out everything but him. "You know how much I hate it when you cry," he says, pressing his lips to mine in a soft kiss. "I like my girls happy and healthy."

"You make us so happy," I whisper, wrapping my arms around his neck.

He smiles at me, his eyes crinkling at the corners. "Then I'm doing my job right, sweet lamb. Making you happy makes me happy. You're an incredible mother and you look like a goddess when you're carrying my kids. I don't want you to ever forget the miracle you're working right now."

"You're too sweet to me."

"Never," he growls.

"I love you so much."

"I know you do. And I love you and our babies more than anything in this world."

He's not exaggerating. He really does love us with his whole heart and soul. He's all in, all the time, holding nothing of himself back from us. He's as dedicated to being a husband and father as he was to his career for so long, more maybe.

I'll be grateful to Vanna, Jimmy, and Le CRV for the rest of my life for bringing him into it. Georgia too. Without her telling him about me, we may never have met. I'd still be returning to a silent house, living vicariously through my books. Instead, I'm living a dream. And every day just gets better and better.

"You going to hush and let me take pictures now?" he asks me.

"Yes."

"Good." He kisses me again, deepening it this time.

"Eww!" Sariah says after a moment, and then giggles when Sage releases me to grab her. He swings her up into his arms, tickling her belly at the same time.

I grab his camera from the nightstand and snap a picture of them. She's screaming with laughter, and he's smiling ear to ear. Their green eyes shine with happiness. Sariah's hair is as wild as mine, and Sage is in an old t-shirt and a pair of sweats. They're both rumpled and messy and somehow even more perfect than ever.

He was right. Being able to look back on moments like this one is better than any magazine spread. This right here...this is living. This is perfection.

And I don't ever want to forget a single moment of it.

Author's Note

If you enjoyed Model Behavior, please consider leaving a review! I appreciate them so much!

Want to read Gray and Camila's story? Ice Breaker is now available! You can also catch up on the rest of the One Night with You series!

Ice Breaker

EXCERPT

"Hello?"

"Gray?"

"Camila," I say, grinning like an idiot. We're leaving for Chicago in a few hours, and I'd resigned myself to the fact that I wasn't going to hear from her before we left. Being wrong doesn't suck. I haven't stopped thinking about her all day.

Either being celibate has done a number on my dick, or he's really into Camila. He keeps popping up and demanding attention. I've already jerked off four times.

"Hi," she mumbles and then huffs out an adorable breath. "I talked to Kelsey."

"You did?" Maybe I won't start that petition after all.

"I did," she confirms. "You're free Friday and Saturday?"

"Yes." Is it wrong to touch my dick again while I'm on the phone with her? Probably. Is it going to stop me? No. Her voice is sexy as hell. I squeeze myself through my sweats, imagining her standing in front of me in that sexy pant suit she was wearing this morning. I'd like to strip it off her with my teeth and lick every inch of skin I unveil. Maybe I shouldn't say that out loud though. Or ask if she's still wearing it.

"Good. I'm sending you a list of things you'll need on Friday. Meet me at the arena at seven in the morning," she says, rushing through it like she's trying to finish this conversation as quickly as humanly possible. I hear the little tremor in her voice though. She's nervous.

Is that a good thing or a bad thing?

I'm not sure, so I settle on a good thing. She wouldn't be nervous to talk to me if she didn't like me at least a little bit, right?

"You'll be gone until Saturday evening."

"We're going somewhere overnight?"

Fuck yeah. This is getting better and better.

"You are," she says. "That list should be coming through now."

She no more says it and my phone buzzes. I pull it away from my ear long enough to glance over the text. Like she said, it's a list.

"Comfortable clothes, sturdy boots, a flask. A compass? Warm socks?" My eyes grow wider the further down the list I go. This does not sound like a sexy overnight trip with my voluptuous publicist.

It sounds like camping. Which, frankly, sounds like the ninth circle of hell.

"You're volunteering with the Boy Scouts."

"What? Why the Boy Scouts?"

"You said you used to be a Scout," she says.

Do I detect a hint of...perverse satisfaction in her voice? I do. I know I do.

"Ah, so this is my punishment for offering to fire you. I assume this was Kelsey's idea?"

"We have a saying, *o peixe morre pela boca*," Camila says in response, though I can hear the amusement in her voice.

"And what does this saying mean?" I ask, making a mental note to make her speak to me in Portuguese forever. It's way more beautiful coming from her than from my translation app.

"Fish die through the mouth. Basically, keep your mouth shut."

"So it was Kelsey." I grin.

"Maybe, maybe not. Why? Is it a problem?"

Yes. Yes, it is absolutely a problem. If bears shit in the woods, they definitely hunt in the woods. And I may be big, but I'm not *fight a fucking bear* big. Not to mention, last time I was in the woods, Jonas damn near shot me. Never go duck hunting with a crazy Canadian.

"No," I lie. "No problem at all."

Ice Breaker is now available!

INSTALOVE BOOK CLUB

The Instalove Book Club is now in session!

Get the inside scoop from your favorite instalove authors, meet new authors to love, and snag freebies and bonus content from featured authors every month. The Instalove Book Club newsletter goes out once per week!

Join now to get your hands on bonus scenes and brand-new, exclusive content from our first six featured authors.

Join the Club: http://instalovebookclub.com

Follow Nichole

Sign-up for Nichole's mailing list at http://authornicholerose.com to stay up to date on all new releases and for exclusive ARC give-aways from Nichole Rose.

Want to connect with Nichole and other readers? Join Nichole Rose's Book Beauties on Facebook!

f
facebook.com/AuthorNicholeRose/

instagram.com/AuthorNicholeRose

twitter.com/AuthNicholeRose

bookbub.com/authors/nichole-rose

tiktok.com/@authornicholerose

More by Nichole Rose

<u>Her Alpha Series</u>
Her Alpha Daddy Next Door
Her Alpha Boss Undercover
Her Alpha's Secret Baby
Her Alpha Protector
Her Date with an Alpha
Her Alpha: The Complete Series

<u>Her Bride Series</u>
His Future Bride
His Stolen Bride
His Secret Bride
His Curvy Bride
His Captive Bride
His Blushing Bride
His Bride: The Complete Series

Claimed Series
Possessing Liberty
Teaching Rowan
Claiming Caroline
Kissing Kennedy
Claimed: The Complete Series

Love on the Clock Series
Adore You
Hold You
Keep You
Protect You
Love on the Clock: The Complete Series

The Billionaires' Club
The Billionaire's Big Bold Weakness
The Billionaire's Big Bold Wish
The Billionaire's Big Bold Woman
The Billionaire's Big Bold Wonder

Playing for Keeps
Cutie Pie
Ice Breaker
Ice Prince
Ice Giant (coming soon)

The Second Generation
A Blushing Bride for Christmas

Love Bites
Come Undone
Dripping Pearls

Silver Spoon MC
The Surgeon
The Heir
The Lawyer
The Prodigy
The Bodyguard

Echoes of Forever
His Christmas Miracle
Taken by the Hitman
Wicked Saint

The Ruined Trilogy
Physical Science
Wrecked

Destination Romance
Romancing the Cowboy
Beach House Beauty

Standalone Titles
A Touch of Summer
Black Velvet
His Secret Obsession
Dirty Boy
Naughty Little Elf
Devil's Deceit
A Bride for the Beast (writing with Fern Fraser)

Easy on Me
Easy Ride
Easy Surrender

One Night with You
Falling Hard
Model Behavior
Learning Curve
Angel Kisses

writing with Loni Ree as Loni Nichole

Dillon's Heart
Razor's Flame
Ryker's Reward (coming soon)
Zane's Rebel (coming soon)

About Nichole Rose

Nichole Rose is a short romance author on the west coast. Her books feature headstrong, sassy women and the alpha males who consume them. From grumpy detectives to country boys with attitude to instalove and over-the-top declarations, nothing is off-limits.

Nichole is sure to have a steamy, sweet story just right for everyone. She fully believes the world is ugly enough without trying to fit falling in love into a one-size-fits-all box. When not writing, Nichole enjoys fine wine, cute shoes, and everything super-natural. She is happily married to the love of her life and is a proud mama to the world's most ridiculous fur-babies.

You can learn more about Nichole and her books at her website .

facebook.com/AuthorNicholeRose/

instagram.com/AuthorNicholeRose

twitter.com/AuthNicholeRose

bookbub.com/authors/nichole-rose

tiktok.com/@authornicholerose